ANN KELLEY is
nearly played cricket for Cornwall
collections of photographs and poem
and some children's fiction, including the award-winning Gussie series. She lives with her second husband and several cats on the edge
of a cliff in Cornwall where they have survived a flood, a landslip,
a lightning strike and the roof blowing off. She runs courses for as-
piring poets at her home, writing courses for medics and medical
students, and speaks about her poetry therapy work with patients
at medical conferences.

FANT

DATE

By the same author:

Born and Bred, Cornwall Books, 1988 (photographs)
Nine Lives, Halsgrove, 1998 (audio book, stories)
The Poetry Remedy, Patten Press, 1999
Paper Whites, London Magazine Editions, 2001 (poems and photographs)
The Burying Beetle, Luath Press, 2005 (a novel)
Sea Front, Truran, 2005 (photographs)
Because We Have Reached That Place, Oversteps Books, 2006 (poems)
The Bower Bird, Luath Press, 2007 (a novel)
Inchworm, Luath Press, 2008 (a novel)
A Snail's Broken Shell, Luath Press, 2010 (a novel)
The Light at St Ives, Luath Press, 2010 (photographs)
Koh Tabu, Oxford University Press, 2010 (a novel)
Lost Girls, Little, Brown US, 2012 (a novel)
Telling the Bees, Oversteps, 2012 (poems)
Last Days in Eden, Luath Press, 2014 (a novel)

Runners

ANN KELLEY

Luath Press Limited

EDINBURGH

www.luath.co.uk

First published 2013
This edition 2014

ISBN: 978-1-910021-16-3

The publisher acknowledges the support of

towards the publication of this book.

The paper used in this book is recyclable.
It is made from low chlorine pulps produced in a low energy,
low emissions manner from renewable forests.

Printed and bound by
ScandBook AB,

Typeset in 9.8 pt Sabon

To Sam and Chloe, with love

CHAPTER ONE

DARKNESS SURROUNDED THEM, a deep velvet black, so that she couldn't see a hand before her. He dragged her wearily through the wood, stumbling and tripping over roots and dead branches, through a shallow stream, their boots heavy now with mud, until they came to a road. It was lighter here where there were no stars but there were fat clouds rushing across the big sky, and the occasional gleam of a segment of orange moon.

She sobbed, her breath broken and ragged. 'Are we there yet, Sid?'

'Nearly. Come on.' He pulled her across the terrifyingly empty space and into more darkness. A military truck coughed and screeched as it slowed to negotiate the bends. The headlights swept across the road.

'Get down!'

It didn't stop. They hadn't been spotted. He switched on the torch briefly to get his bearings. Between densely packed trees and shrubs he saw a pile of abandoned building materials including a length of pipe about three metres long and of a diameter sufficient for the two to stand upright. She was unable to walk any further.

He picked her up and carried her into the tunnel.

'We're safe here.'

Lo woke with sun flickering through high branches, dappling the leafy floor outside their new den. Sid was good at making dens.

He had made three that she remembered. One was a brick-walled roofless coal shed, which she liked because she could see the stars, but when it rained they got wet. The next den was a smelly old chicken house, but the feathers and dirt made her sneeze and they were discovered and chased out by a gang of kids who threw stones at them. They had had trouble finding another safe place. There were many empty buildings in the city, windows smashed, contents trashed or looted. But other kids had taken them as their own. Eventually, after walking all day through dusty deserted suburbs, hiding whenever they saw anyone, when they were exhausted and frantic for shelter they came across an old bus in a burnt-out depot full of very young kids who shared their drinking water with them.

Teams of them went out each day to scavenge for food. Sid was good at it and the little kids wanted them to stay. That was the best refuge and lasted ages and ages, at least two weeks. She'd liked it there because there were other little girls and they played tea parties with her and she was allowed to be Mother and pour the tea. They admired her fairyprincessdress. It was all pink and she liked to twirl round in it and show off her frilly pants. But a gang of youths had found them and thrown the younger ones out, threatening them with the Reducers, and they had had to run with only a small backpack containing several tins of baked beans, a can of Labmeat, a tin opener, a half-empty water bottle, matches, and the stained photo of their parents that Sid carried in the pocket of his baggies. And their IDs, carried in a waterproof pouch on a string around his neck.

Lo had cried bitter tears at leaving the other bus children, who had scattered and disappeared like scuttling rats.

She wept at lots of things these days: like when soldiers had pushed her and Sid into one truck and Mammy and Dadda into another.

'Mammy, Mammy,' Lo had screamed. But there were lots of screaming children in their truck.

Sid had tried to comfort her. He said Mammy and Dadda were going to a Sunshine Camp and they would see them soon. But she had cried so much her head hurt.

She wept when later the same day, after they had run away

from the broken-down truck, Sid had thrown away her armband with the yellow sunshine picture on it.

'I like it, Sid. Why did you do that?'

'Because!' he said. And her sobs began again. 'Shh, don't cry, Lo.' He had hugged her to him, aware of how her hair was sticky and unwashed, her arms covered in scabs and grime. They were hiding in a large wheelie bin full of smelly rubbish. No one would look for them in there.

He had thrown away his own armband too. They'd all had to wear them in the ghetto.

Most people there were very young or very old, disabled or chronically sick, derelict or pregnant. There was a football pitch, a soup kitchen and even a prison in the ghetto, but no one was allowed out. It was for their own safety, they were told, because life outside the ghetto was chaotic, hazardous, lawless. The news-sheets announced a relocation programme to transport them to a place where they could be looked after.

However, Sid knew better now. He knew from what he had witnessed and what he'd heard along the way, that ghetto people were not going to be cared for. The opposite was true. He'd seen with his own eyes soldiers bludgeoning those who didn't go quietly. His mother had been dragged away and his father had been lifted from his wheelchair and thrown roughly into the back of the truck.

His mam had been right. She had heard rumours from the other ghetto women and had tried to warn his dad weeks before the razor-wire went up. In the cramped two-roomed accommodation they shared he couldn't help overhearing their midnight rows.

'We could get out in the night. Start walking. Go west. To my folks. Sid and I could push your wheelchair.'

'Don't be stupid, woman, it's a hundred miles or more. Haven't heard from them in years. Don't even know if they are still alive.'

'But we can't just wait to be taken away. It's like the Nazis. They aren't going to look after us, they are going to take us to Reduction camps. And we're going meekly to our deaths.' She sobbed into her hands.

'It's vicious gossip, don't listen to it.'

Sid had tried not to listen. Instead he'd read his book under the bedclothes. *The Life of Isambard Kingdom Brunel.* He'd disappeared into another world: a world of huge bridges, of grand buildings and tunnels under the Thames.

Before their life in the ghetto, the bridges over the Tamar had been demolished to keep out refugees. He had been on the river bank to watch with excitement the huge structures fall creaking and crashing into the water. His father, who had worked on the maintenance of the Isambard Kingdom Brunel Railway Bridge for most of his working life, had wept openly.

Their new den was a dry tunnel. Sid had been hard at work already, gathering bits and pieces. They sat on plastic cartons.

'I'm hungry.' She scratched her scalp.

'You're always hungry, Lo.' He opened a tin of baked beans and gave it to her. She scooped out the tomato goo with her fingers and sucked them clean.

'Where are we?'

'Roundabout.'

'Where are the rides?'

'Nah, not that sort of roundabout. It's like an island, but instead of water around it there's road.'

'Is it the country?' (She couldn't yet sound her r's, so it sounded like *countwy*.)

'Sort of.'

'Is it safe?'

'Yeah, it's safe.'

'Why is it?'

'Just is. Come on, we've work to do.'

Sid enjoyed building things. He wanted to be a structural engineer, like his dad had been before his accident. This, he thought, is a miniature version of the Thames Tunnel that his hero had helped to build when he was just twenty. Only six years older than Sid. He pretended that he was working with Brunel as he yanked, tugged and manhandled a sheet of corrugated plastic to block one end of the tunnel, then disguised it with dead branches.

'There you are, Sidney, very well made.'

'Thank you, sir.' It comforted Sid, to imagine that he wasn't

alone in this task.

The other end of the den was already hidden by dense bushes and a tree trunk that had fallen close by.

It was like a cave, a wild creature's lair.

'Are there wild things?' Lo was scared.

'Like what?'

'I don't know. Wild things what roar and eat people.'

'Nah. We're all right.'

'No rats?' Lo had seen many large rats in the city and she was frightened of what they could do. One of the bus girls had said a rat as big as a cat had crawled over her in her bed and roared at her.

'No rats.' Sid's experience of wildlife was limited to the moan of feral pigeons, the screech of rats, the rich scent of city fox, and his body's own wildlife – nits and fleas, and more recently, lice.

'Can I explore?'

'I'll come with you first time, okay? Then we'll both know the way home, won't we, eh?'

'Is it our den, now, Sid?'

'For a bit, yeah.'

Being careful not to show themselves to the open road, it took about twenty minutes to walk round close to the perimeter of the roundabout, climbing over fallen trees and pushing through brambles and shrubs with a stout stick.

'Sid, my feet hurt, Sid,' Lo whimpered. Not surprising, he thought. He still couldn't believe that they got this far. They had walked over sixty miles in the last ten days or so, following minor roads and disused railway tracks, sleeping in abandoned buildings and old train stations, always heading west. And she was only little.

Lo's legs were already covered in scratches and bites, so the thorns didn't bother her much. But her precious dress tore easily and she was upset by its every new imperfection.

'Where are we going, Sid?'

'Find Gramps and Grumps.'

'Why?'

'They want to see us, that's why.' He doubted that Grumps

would be happy to see them, but maybe his grandfather would. If he could find them. A town with a 'z' in it. He had no choice, they were his only hope. No way could he look after Lo and himself for long. They both needed somewhere safe to stay. He daren't think about what had happened to his parents. He wasn't ready to face the horrific possibilities that flitted through his mind.

'But Sid, how will Mammy and Dadda know where we are?'

'Don't start, Lo. Watch out.' He lifted her over a prickly bush. 'Why don't you tuck your dress in your pants.'

'Don't want to.'

'No water, but it's good here,' he announced. They had come back to where they had started, a yellow flowering gorse bush and a clump of tall teasels behind a large arrow sign.

'What's it called?'

'What do you mean?

'What's its name, the roundybout?

'Don't know. We'll give it a name, shall we?' He pushed a stray lock of matted hair behind her ear.

Lo scratched her leg and frowned. 'Fairy Island.'

'Nah. Don't be stupid.' He hit at a thick clump of branches to make a way through back to the den.

'I'm not stupid. And you're a pooey-face.' Lo paused, looking up through the mass of leaves at the cloudy sky. 'Green Island'.

The roundabout was a thick mass of shrubs, bushes and tall trees and supported a small zoo of wildlife, though nothing that wanted to eat children. Lo was right. It was a green island.

The resident badger was aware of their presence and the barn owl in the high tree had heard them arrive as he was delicately eviscerating a rat.

The badger was digging for worms in the warm earth when the humans arrived. She lifted her heavy striped head and sniffed the air. They smelled bad but not in a dangerous way. The skinny fox who had his den on the roundabout was roaming far away.

CHAPTER TWO

AT THE FIRST GLIMMER of dawn Sid left Lo sleeping in the tunnel. He had made them a bed with a polythene sheet covered in dead grass and dry leaves, a huge pile that smelt of earth and autumn. Over the last weeks they had acquired the habit of snatching the blessed oblivion of sleep when they could, day or night.

He hid behind one of several curved metal barriers that edged the island and listened to the two roads within his sight for a few minutes. Nothing came or went, only a gang of twenty or more motorbikes going too fast, leather-clad riders leaning at dangerous angles around the bends. The roar they made was scary and made his stomach churn. He went back to the tunnel to check that his little sister hadn't been disturbed by the racket. She was snoring softly. Nothing woke Lo. Mam said she was always *a good baby*.

A pair of buzzards circled high in the white hot sky, mewing harshly. He made a dash across the road into the wood, his stout stick at the ready for whoever or whatever challenged him. In this case it was only brambles.

After about a kilometre he passed an abandoned piggery, five pens still faintly smelling of pig – a sweet meaty scent – (another possible den, he filed into his brain for the future). Nothing in them – only a gnarled tree growing through one; rusted feeding troughs outside. The yard tap squeaked when he turned it, but no water flowed. A hundred metres away he found what he was looking for: fresh water. A flooded quarry. The sides were steep, the water level low. He walked around its edge, climbing trees to get a better look at what was ahead. He watched as a fish touched the lid of the water and sent out ripples. Beyond the concentric circles he saw a moulded fibreglass dinghy tied to a short wooden pier. Crouching, he made himself small, picked his nose thoughtfully, and watched for a few minutes to make sure there was no one there. He climbed down and continued around the edge until he came to wooden steps to the pier. Fixed to a pole was an orange lifebelt.

Filling up the bottle with the greenish water, he waited for the silt to settle and drank deeply, refilled it and screwed the lid on. He stayed under the pier for a long time, watching branches dipping into the water, a cloud of mosquitoes shimmering in the sun. A movement startled him. A grey squirrel leapt from one tree to another like a slow motion film, feathered tail flickering over its back.

Sid had never been anywhere this quiet. Tranquillity. That was the word for it. There was no menace in the silence, only the sounds of birds and insects, the hiss of wind in leaves, the smell of water and green things. Reflections of clouds passed beneath him as he looked longingly at the boat. Walking all the way around the quarry he looked for signs of life, but saw no paths, no broken twigs, nothing to indicate that anyone had been there for many months. He saw a bright green grasshopper climbing up a tall grass. He knelt to watch a spider mend the web that he had inadvertently broken as he stepped through it. A dancing pair of brown speckled butterflies flickered in the corner of his eye. The scent of honeysuckle soothed him. He had no idea that there was so much wildlife in the countryside. A ladybird landed on his hand, and he examined it closely as it crawled up his arm. Red and black, like a small armoured car, he thought. Seven spots. 'Fly away ladybird, fly away home…' he couldn't remember the words of the nursery rhyme. Something about a fire and losing its children. Even ladybirds had a hard time. Obediently, it folded back its red and black carapace, opened its wings and flew off.

Fly away home. He would never see *his* home again. He sniffed hard.

There were oars in the bottom of the boat, and a dark puddle of rainwater in which mosquito larvae wriggled. He got in, rocking the dinghy, put the oars in the rowlocks, untied the rope and rowed off into the middle of the water.

He'd never done it before, but he soon got the hang of it. Now, the muscles on his arms felt stretched and good. It was such a normal boy thing to do. It was a long time since he'd done normal. It took him some time to circle the flooded gravel pit. A hatch of dragonflies shimmered above the water. A wood pigeon cooed sadly. Woo, woo, woo-oo.

He reluctantly tied the boat to the pier again and started off on the journey back to the roundabout. Looking inside the pigpens once more, he kicked at the soiled straw and found an empty plastic bucket. He sniffed inside it. Satisfied, he put the handle over his arm and hurried back, suddenly anxious that Lo had woken and wandered off.

Lo was awake, listless, but her eyes brightened when she saw him. He thought again how grubby she looked. Tears had made white tracks down her cheeks and neck. And it occurred to him that he was also caked with dirt. They hadn't bathed or washed since fleeing the city. He still couldn't believe their luck: the overcrowded truck breaking down a mile or so outside the ghetto. He, Lo, and several other kids had made good their escape before the driver could stop them.

'Where were you?' she accused.

'Here, drink this.' She sipped at the water, grimaced and spat.

'Gritty?'

'Yes.'

'Take your sock off.'

'Why?' She only had one sock and she was fond of it.

'Give it to me, go on.'

She reluctantly removed a pink and blue flowered wellie and the filthy white sock and sniffed it.

'Pooh, smelly feet.' Lo giggled.

'Maybe it's not such a good idea,' said Sid, and reached inside his backpack for his spare football socks, which were slightly less grubby than his little sister's.

All they had on them was what they were wearing when the

soldiers came. Sid had just got back from football practice and Lo was wearing the same thing she had worn all weekend – wellies and a pink net tutu dress and wings. The wings had long gone, torn to shreds by thorns soon after they reached open country, and the wire frame had been abandoned days ago. Thinking about it, he should probably have saved the wire. You never knew when it would come in useful.

'Hold it open, like this,' he said. He poured a little of the gritty water through a football sock into the water bottle and she drank the vaguely filtered water.

'Still bitty,' she grimaced.

'I know what will do it.' Without asking, he took the underskirt of her pink net dress in both hands and ripped off a strip.

She wailed, 'No, Sid!'

'Shh! It's all right, see, makes no difference. Can't see it, can you?' she looked as if she was going to cry. Her mouth went down at the corners and her lips quivered. He put the fine gauze over the neck of the bottle, told Lo to hold it steady, and gradually poured the silty water through it. It works, he thought, pleased with himself.

'Now try it.'

'I found a lake,' he said as she quenched her thirst.

'What's a lake?'

'Swimming pool.'

'Swimming pool? Go now! Go now! Go now!'

A lone black-headed gull sat on the lake, its tiny wake snagging the silk of the calm water. Alarmed, it took off when it saw them, diamonds dripping from its webbed feet.

Sid tied her to the pier and put the lifebelt over her head and around her waist. She splashed around the sides of the boat, barefoot, in just her pants, squealing with excitement and the cold. 'I'm swimming. I'm swimming. Look at me, Sid.'

'Shh! Someone might hear.'

He dunked their clothes in the water, swooshed them around, wrung them out and hung them on bushes to dry. Sun glinted in a million stars on the water. They lay in the shade of a rowan and slept. When he woke he was surprised at how blonde she was.

He'd forgotten. Under the filth and grime they were both tanned. He shook her gently to wake her.

'Want a boat ride, Sid. Can I have a boat ride?' She rubbed her eyes with the backs of her hands.

'Another time, all right?'

'Why not now?'

'Because.' It was what his mother would have said. They drank again and dressed in their damp clothes.

'It's all floppy, Lo complained. Her fairyprincessdress had once been stiff with starch.

'Nah, it's nice. Clean, yeah?'

'Yeah. Smells like sweeties.'

A blackbird fluttered past them, chittering in alarm. The dusty branches quivered in the light breeze.

'Is this our new den?'

'Nah, roundabout's safer.'

'I like it here, Sid.'

He liked it, too. But the boat must belong to someone. That was Sid's worry. If they camped here, they were more likely to be discovered. The roundabout was a better bet.

'Put your boots on.'

'Don't want to.'

'Don't start, Lo.' He put her wet sock in his backpack and picked up her boots.

'My feet hurt,' she yelled.

'Shh! Okay, don't wear them. You'll have to carry them, then.'

He set off with Lo limping behind, whining softly, a boot under each arm.

They cut across a field, bordered by tall stone hedges.

'What's that?' she asked. She had trodden on a dry cowpat.

'I think it must be cow shit.'

'You swore,' she said disapprovingly. 'What's a cow?'

'Farm animal. Before Labmeat there used to be hundreds of cows, sheep and pigs in the fields. Farmers fed them until they were fat, then killed them and we ate them.'

'Yuk!'

'We got milk from the cows. Remember milk? White stuff? Ah

no, you had soy milk, didn't you? I had real cow's milk when I was little.'

He started singing to her:

'Old MacDonald had a farm, E I E I O
And on that farm he had a cow, E I E I O.
With a moo moo here
A moo moo there…
Here a moo, there a moo,
Everywhere a moo moo,
Old MacDonald had a farm, E I E I O.'

'Remember, Lo?'

She shook her head. 'What's it like?'

'What?'

'Cow milk?'

'Dunno. Warm, chalky, nice.'

'Chalky?'

'Yeah, like liquid chalk.'

'Yuk! I like soy stuff.'

'Anyway, there's next to no farm animals anymore. Same as pets.'

'There's rabbits,' Lo said.

'Yeah, and birds.'

'In books there's animoos.'

'Yeah, in books.'

'Cawwy me,' Lo implored. He yanked her up onto his shoulders once more. He had carried her it seemed forever like this.

Back at the den she asked, 'Can we have a barbecue, Sid?'

'They'll see the smoke, stupid.'

'I'm not stupid. Pooey-face!' She frowned at him, pouting until she felt a bubble coming. She liked blowing bubbles.

They ate another tin of baked beans between them. He would have to find more food soon.

'Read me a story, Sid.' Her eyelids were drooping.

'Haven't gotta book, have we?'

'Make a story then,' she begged as she lay on the bed of leaves, the limp net skirt in a circle around her. She bent a leg, held one foot close to her face and picked at it.

He sighed deeply and lay down next to her. 'Onceaponatime, onceaponatime,' he gabbled, frowning, 'there were two kids who ran away from home.'

'Why did they run away?'

'Listen, will yer? Or I won't tell you a story.'

'Want the Billy Goat story! Billy Goat story! Billy Goat story!' She waved her feet in the air.

'Don't start, Lo.' He needed to relax, to sleep.

'My feet hurt.' It was as if she was almost apologising.

He sighed and looked at the foot she waved in his face. There were burst blisters on her heel and toes. He felt a pang of sympathy. Poor little kid, she had been so stoic. He had been embarrassed when Mam got pregnant with Lo when he'd been a shy and sensitive nine-year-old. He hadn't wanted to think about his parents having sex. And he hadn't had much to do with Lo while she was a baby. He had his own life to lead – football, school, his dreams of being an engineer. He had got to know her well really only in the last few weeks. She was amazingly adaptable, accepting the drastic changes in their life as if it was completely normal. At first she had cried for her parents, but now she seemed to have almost forgotten them.

He felt a deep affection for his little sister. He had got them this far, he would make sure that she was safe. He'd never had to look after anyone or anything in his life. But he would never forget his mam's words as they had been taken away –

'Look after my baby, Sid, keep her safe.'

Lo wished she still had her bit of blanket that she used to rub on her nose when she was sleepy. She couldn't remember how it had been lost. She picked at her net dress as she sucked her soggy thumb.

She was asleep before he had to think of what happened next in the Billy Goats Gruff story.

Darkness came like a friend.

As he was slipping into sleep a dreadful noise came, like monsters murdering each other. Sid's heartbeat quickened. He didn't breathe, he sat up straight, watching for lights. The angry yowls stopped. He sat there for some minutes, listening, watching, tense.

They slept. The temperature had dropped to a comfortable twenty-six degrees. This autumn was even hotter than usual. Leaves still hung limp on the trees. Grass was the colour of sand.

They hadn't noticed the paw prints of badger and the spoor of the fox that had investigated the den in their absence. The badger had a sett in the middle of the roundabout. Her tunnel went down and under the road, and had several exits in the woods on the other side. She returned, bad-tempered and sore after the battle with a young male. He had come off worse and had lumbered off, nursing wounds to his face and shoulder.

Many rabbits had burrows on the roundabout, and night and day they gathered on the edge to feed on grass, noses and whiskers twitching. The pair of buzzards kept watch overhead and one suddenly swooped to pick off a kit. Before sunrise the ghost-white owl flew back low over the road from vole territory on the other side.

Sid woke, checked that Lo was still deeply asleep, then explored the whole of the roundabout. It was a low circular mound. There were only bushes and trees, no other piles of building materials. But it was thickly planted and he felt strangely safe. It was like an island, a desert island. Shady and cool. Green. No one would think of looking for them there. And the proximity of fresh water was ideal, not too close, not too far away. They could rest up here while Lo's blisters healed. He tunnelled through the leaves and tangled branches, his fingers stained purple by the blackberries he ate as he came across them. There were nuts on the leafy earth. He didn't know what they were, but he knew he had had some one Christmas. He cracked open the shell between two stones and ate a hazelnut. He searched and found more. His stomach was cramping. He had to find more food. When he got back, Lo was sitting up and rubbing her eyes.

'I got you some berries, look.'

She took a blackberry, spitting out the seeds.

'I'm going to leave you here and find us something to eat.'

'Why? Why can't I come?'

'Because.' His mam was always saying that, and it had always irritated him. He fought to find the words to persuade Lo with a sensible explanation. 'You're going to stay because you've got sore feet. Don't go near the road, yeah? In case someone sees you. Stay here. Eat the blackberries.'

He wasn't worried that Lo would stray off the roundabout. Since leaving the ghetto he had instilled in her a fear of empty spaces, of the openness of the road, aware that a small figure crossing could be seen for miles. And he *was* concerned about the state of her feet. The blisters needed to heal before she walked any great distance.

He shrugged on the empty backpack. He left her the bottle of water and the torch, in case. In case he didn't get back before dark. In case he didn't get back at all. He had thought about tying her to a tree but decided against it, in case he didn't ever get back to set her free. And anyway, it was a long walk to the quarry to fetch the rope.

'You know how to do it. Like that. See?'

He switched on the torch and switched it off again. Don't turn it on unless you have to,' he warned. 'And don't make a noise or someone will find you.'

'Okay. Kiss bye-bye.' She held her cheek up to his lips. He sighed and pecked it briefly.

'I lost my wellies, Sid,' she whispered.

'You didn't! Where?' He looked around in vain. 'Why didn't you tell me before?'

Her lips started to quiver.

'Never mind, don't cry. I'll find them.'

He tried to remember when she had had them last. She had been carrying them when they left the lake. Had she put them down in the field where the cowpats were? He'd have to go back and look. A Reducer could find them. Or the TA. They would know then that there was a small child nearby.

'Be good, be safe,' she said.

It was what their mam had always said when he set off to the ghetto school. He'd hated school. Now he longed for those lost days when he had gazed out of the dusty windows, bored out of his mind, yawning in the airless room that smelt of feet and chalk and adolescent sweat.

'You too,' he said, frowning. 'I'll be back soon as poss. Eat the beans if you get hungry and don't go near the road. And Lo – if someone comes, tell them you're eight, Okay?'

'I'm eight,' she said, doubtfully. 'Why must I say I'm eight when I'm only five and a half?'

'Just say you're eight.'

It was hopeless, he knew. She was obviously very young, and anyway, once they checked her microchip they would know exactly how old she was.

He opened the can and left the lid on.

'Don't cut yourself on the lid,' he warned her. 'Open it with a stick, okay? Like this.'

He showed her how to prise up the lid, and pushed it down again. Having second thoughts, he removed the lid completely and buried it. He couldn't risk Lo cutting herself while he wasn't there.

He blew a kiss at the forlorn little figure in the limp tutu.

CHAPTER THREE

AS HE REACHED the dry-stone hedge of the cowpat field and went to climb over, he heard someone whistling. Not the cheerful tunes his dad used to make before his accident, but a mournful, monotonous sound of one repeated phrase.

He peered over the hedge. A raggedy man, grey head bent, was on the far side of the field, a baseball cap in his hand. Sid's heart beat faster. He had to get to the wellies before the man spotted them. The pink and blue boots stood out from the surrounding brown of the parched grass.

How could he not see them? What was he looking for? Sid saw the man bend and pluck a small round mushroom and put it in the baseball cap.

He slipped down into the field while the forager's back was turned and flattened himself on the earth. He crawled slowly on his belly in the direction of the boots. The man was headed towards him now.

How could he not see the boots?

But he was concentrating hard on his quest for food, looking only at the immediate surroundings, searching for the horse mushrooms that appeared each morning before the dew had disappeared. Sliding carefully towards his goal, Sid held his breath while the man, unaware of the boy a few metres away, gathered his harvest of fungi.

As the man turned to pluck a particularly good specimen, Sid made a mad dash for the boots, snatched them up and ran for the stone hedge, leaping over it triumphantly.

The man looked up and yelled, 'Oi, kid, what you at?'

Sid ignored him and ran as fast as he could.

'Hayle 3 miles', the sign said, with the Cornish place name *Heyl* in brackets. Someone had crossed out the name and spray-painted HELL over it. No vehicles passed him. They mostly seemed to travel by dark, the Territorial Army. He passed a grey low building. Derelict. No skeletons inside, only the smell of old blood, like the taste of metal on his tongue. He took a poker from the blackened fireplace and tucked it into the belt of his baggies. No food in the cupboard; the fridge was full of black mould and furry stuff growing on plates, like alien green and purple flowers. He tried the taps. Nothing. Only rust. In one bedroom he found a grubby cot blanket and a knitted toy rabbit. He nearly went without them, but thinking of Lo, stuffed them into the bag. There were no clothes in the wardrobes.

The skeleton of a cat was curled in an armchair by the stove. It looked beautiful, he thought, its sharp teeth intact. The fur, lying around it, as if it had shaken it off, had turned to grey dust. He remembered a ginger cat, called Tiddles, when he was as small as Lo, before Lo was born, but it had been taken in the DARP – the Domestic Animal Reduction Program – and Mam said she could never have another unless they moved to the country. She had always wanted to move to the country, but Dad said they weren't allowed pets in the country either, and anyway no way would he move to the sticks.

A rank smell came from the sitting room where someone or something had shat in a corner; the sleepy buzz of fat blue flies; dead moths on the window ledge.

He took a swig of water from the bottle and had a look in a shed – sticky cobwebs, a spade, a garden fork, wire, gardening gloves, a rusty lawnmower, a hank of rope, a can of weed killer. Setting off again along the road, he kept close to the verge, ready to leap into a ditch or bushes if he saw a movement anywhere. But there were only crows coughing hoarsely in trees, a flock of starlings swirling like a horizontal tornado along the hedge tops in the distance. A field of poppies glowed under the grey sky. Like his mother he had always wanted to live in the country. 'Now I am. Funny, innit?' he said to himself. It occurred to him that his blue T-shirt, on was probably as visible for miles as the poppies were. He tore it off and put it in the bag. At this rate there'd be no room for food, he thought. He should have hidden the boots somewhere and picked them up on his way back to the den.

Filling leaf plates with blackberries and acorns, Lo sang to herself a song she half remembered, something about teddy bears and a picnic. *If you go down the woods today.* She ate the berries and licked her fingers. She tried an acorn but it was too hard so she spat it out. Her head itched and she scratched it with torn fingernails. She picked off a ripe scab from her arm and it bled, so she licked it. Wandering close to the den, she found a bit of short dead bough with a knob on the end and called it Rosebud. She made a dock-leaf dress for her and scolded her for getting it dirty. Back at the den she and Rosebud had a tea party.

'Would you like a biscuit?' she asked her doll, pushing a berry at where a mouth might be. Used to entertaining herself, she played bus kids with Rosebud, plus other twig dolls. She told them to be quiet or they'd be caught.

'Look out, they're coming to get you,' she whispered, dropping gravel on them. Leaf plasters were applied to their horrible injuries. She cuddled up with Rosebud on the carpet of leaves and told her a story about three goats and a bridge with a monster under it. It had always frightened her – the monster wanting to eat the Billy Goats Gruff, but she had asked her mother for it time and again. The five-year-old couldn't remember what had happened to the billy goats or the monster. It was something she didn't want to think about. At the same time, she wanted to know the ending. Sid would make a happy ending.

'And they all lived happy-ev-after,' she called out, triumphantly, forgetting that she needed to keep quiet or Sid would be cross.

A robin leaned on match-stick legs from a bough and watched the child for a moment, and sang its evening song, a melancholy, sweet melody. Lo curled up on the leaves and switched the torch on and off, on and off, shining it onto her hand, trying to see through to the other side. She fell asleep after a while, and a little later the torch battery died.

Sid's foot hurt – a blister. He removed his trainers and shoved them in the backpack, thinking that if they had laces instead of Velcro he could have tied them around his neck like a soldier would have done. What luck that he had managed to save the backpack! Lo's boots stuck out of it. He marched along the cracked tarmac, the poker resting on one shoulder like a rifle. If only he had a real gun! He stopped every now and then to listen for traffic. Nothing. Then the unmistakable whir of a helicopter. Whup, whup, whup. He dashed into the ditch and crouched under a thick bush. The helicopter swept low over the road coming from the direction of the town. He waited until he could no longer hear it before getting out and continuing his journey. He hadn't seen or heard an airplane since he was little. Only military helicopters now.

A boarded-up service station was the only building he passed. Torn paper on a news-stand proclaimed:

MORE FLOODS.
MANY DEAD AND MISSING.
EASTERN COUNTIES INUNDATED.

On another tattered news-sheet, months old, were the words:

NO MORE OIL! And in smaller type: LOOTERS SHOT.

He knew all about that. Looters shot in the streets; shops boarded up; curfews; tear gas, and then the awful day when everything changed. Every time it came into his mind he had a panicky feeling as if his heart was about to burst. It was easier not to think about it. It was quite easy after a while, blocking it out. He could pretend it just hadn't happened.

Afterwards, they'd been in a TA truck with several other kids, all crying and wetting themselves, if not worse, and after about an hour of terror the vehicle broke down. And when the soldier had got out to see what was wrong, Sid had told Lo to be very quiet and they had got out and run away and hidden in a large wheelie bin. He tore off the armbands with the sunshine motif and buried them in the garbage.

They had stayed in the rubbish bin until it was dark. Lo had sobbed with shock and fear and he had cuddled her, even though she smelled of rotting food and urine. Neither of them smelled too good. He had no idea where they were. A long way from home, that was sure. Not in the ghetto. And he *had* looked after her. As his mother had implored him to.

He found them safe places to sleep, hid during the day in empty buildings, then in that old bus with the ferals. Runners. Surviving. That was the first time he had heard the word Runners.

At night, in the dark, the bus kids had told their stories – how their parents had tried to hide them from the soldiers, and the screams when they had been taken. The barbaric scenes they had witnessed. Shootings, beatings. All the children cried out in their sleep.

One night, when he was scavenging in a burnt-out Labmeat store, he nearly bumped into a thin girl of about sixteen. She was wrapped in a dark cloak with a hood. She was pretty, with large dark eyes, a dimple in her chin, and as the hood slipped he could see that her head was shaved.

'Where you from then?' she asked him, eyeing him up and down, not worried, now that she could see that he was only a skinny kid. Not a lad to be scared of.

'East of here. You?'

'Rather not say.'

'Oh! Where are you going?' he asked.

'Rather not say,' she whispered, looking around anxiously. They had carried on searching the aisles.

'How old are you?' she asked when they met in the next aisle.

'Fourteen. You?'

'Small for fourteen, aren't you?' she said, not unkindly.

He was silent, humiliated. This was the first girl who had spoken to him since he had started to notice girls. He *didn't* look fourteen. He was small, like his dad. Skinny but fast. He'd always come first at the hundred metres at school. He stood tall, fixed a grim look on his face, trying to look older.

'I *am* fourteen,' he said, firmly, as he looked into her dark eyes.

She smiled. 'I'm sixteen. You're all right. I'm the one who shouldn't be here.' She shifted the damaged box of out-of-date Labmeat she had found so that it sat less awkwardly under her arm.

'What do you mean?'

'Don't you know? The Population Reduction Programme? Only kids between eight and fourteen are allowed to live in Fortress Kernow now. And only the fit ones.

'But why?' he'd asked. 'I don't understand.'

'Too many people, aren't there! Reducers are rounding up Runners and transporting them to the camps.'

'Reducers?'

'They work for the TA, the soldiers, and chase the Runners, like me. Why are you running, then?'

'Got my little sister to look after, haven't I! She's five.' He suddenly felt aware of the responsibility he had taken on. And full of rage. Furious that his father had not taken notice of Mam's warnings.

'Well, good luck, Titch! See ya.' She held his head, kissed him on the mouth and ran off.

Confused, happy, he looked towards where she had run, but couldn't see her.

Too late he thought of other things he should have asked her.

Why were kids between eight and fourteen allowed to stay in Fortress Kernow?

Where was she running to?

Would she be safe?

He hoped so. He tentatively licked his lips, tasting her.

Images came unbidden into his mind, especially when he was trying to sleep: in a vain attempt to save their pets from the DARP some people had thrown their dogs out to fend for themselves. Stray dogs found other strays and formed packs. They were shot on sight. Sid saw again the spilling guts, heard the yelping and dying sighs of a mob of terriers and mongrels.

But the things he couldn't rid his brain of were Dad's helplessness that last day, and his mam's face, the O her mouth made, the look in her eyes as she was dragged away. He would never forget that.

CHAPTER FOUR

HE WAS PLEASED about finding the flooded quarry. Maybe he could catch fish in it. Fishing had been banned since years before The Emergency – he knew that from school. There weren't enough fish left in the sea. Man had taken too many of them. And now the acid water was killing them so they were in danger of extinction. But this wasn't the sea, it was a lake. He could make a fishing line and hang it over the side of the boat like he had seen people do on the telly, before the electricity had gone. Before the ghetto. He thought of all the useless stuff he had learned at school – Maths, Mandarin, Geography. Why hadn't his father taught him useful stuff, like how to make a camp, and fishing? Why hadn't he realised things were going terribly wrong and got them somewhere safe? He was a useless father. He hated him. He was glad he had had the accident. Sid's eyes filled and his throat tightened. He wanted to scream out loud but was afraid to in case someone heard.

'*What would you do, sir?*' he silently asked Isambard Kingdom Brunel.

'*You are doing very well, my little friend. Don't worry. Live for the day, and you will survive.*'

He kicked a pebble along the road, dribbled it, did a tricky back-flip, became a football ace and promptly lost it in the ditch. A little brown bird flapped squeaking from the ditch into a hedge. Sid did some karate moves as he walked, slashing the air with his hands, killing with one blow. He'd done judo too, but preferred karate. In his and Lo's bedroom in the ghetto he'd had a poster showing the six striking surfaces of the hand. It occurred to him that he would never see the room again. It was such a dreadful thought that he couldn't manage to think beyond it. Frowning, he flicked his hair out of his eyes.

His stomach rumbled and he had a sudden yearning for porridge. He imagined he was eating a bowl of creamy porridge with honey on. Saliva filled his mouth. He picked blackberry seeds from between his teeth and sucked them.

His back was burning. He took out his T-shirt and flung it around his shoulders but it kept slipping off so he wrapped it around his hot head, like a turban. A khaki T-shirt was on the top of his wish list, second only to a gun. He would be invisible, camouflaged like a real soldier.

In the distance a shimmering shape hovered above the tarmac, and he slipped into the shallow ditch again. The drone of a vehicle became louder, a heavy drone, like millions of bees. It was an armoured car, camouflaged with zigzagged yellow and dark green paint, narrow slits as windows. It drove past fast and he waited until he could no longer hear it before he unfolded himself and crawled back onto the road. He whistled a tune he had heard a long time ago. Whistling made him feel happy. He was on an adventure, he told himself, going to save himself and his little sister, going to find Mam and Dad. Rescue them. They'd all live in the countryside with his grandparents, and Dad would be able to walk again and teach him to fish. And there'd be electricity again, and the telly, and air-conditioning. And they'd have porridge and toast for breakfast every day, and Mam would cook pizza. Not just on birthdays.

But he knew it was all a dream.

Sid remembered going with Gramps years ago to his sloping GM veggie plot overlooking a bay. There was a small rocky island with a castle on top. Or had he imagined that? It didn't sound feasible, more like something from a book. But he did remember gulls following a plough, gleaming white against the dark soil, their harsh laughter. What he *could* do was find his grandparents. They lived by the seaside, the Far West, somewhere or other with a 'z' in the name. That was his quest.

But first he had to find food. Potatoes, maybe. He knew where potatoes came from – not only in plastic bags from the market. He wasn't stupid. He took to the fields and pulled at the leaves of every crop he came across. He dug with his hands and the poker at the dry earth, wishing he had the spade. Large white pearls hung by threads to the roots. He was pleased with himself. He could do this. He dug up a few more small potatoes. How do you turn these hard objects into mash or chips?

The ploughed ridges caused him to stumble several times. Blackberries glistened in the hedges, blue-bellied flies hanging from them. He ate as many berries as he could. He yanked at a cabbage in another field, twisting it and slashing at the stalk with the knife. His fingers slid over squashed caterpillars that smelt of rotten cabbage. It must be after ten. At home he would have been in bed by now, reading with a torch under the duvet, Mam and Dad in the next room, arguing, Lo asleep. He could see windmills on the hillside and the square tower of a church a couple of fields away. The setting sun lit the windows as if they were on fire. If there was a church there must be houses and maybe a soup kitchen like in the city. His stomach rumbled at the thought.

He crept up to the squat bungalow, keeping low. The domestic windmill hummed in the breeze. He left his backpack in a hedge, but thought twice and went back for it, and climbed over a wall to the rear that was covered in clambering yellow and orange flowers with round leaves. There was an open window to the kitchen through which he could hear the soft murmur of two people. He didn't look in. Instead, he went round to the front door, still keeping low and close to the wall. A small dog barked from inside the bungalow. Sid froze and crouched down by bushes. The air smelled of earth and perfume. Like his mam. White flowers glowed in the gathering gloom. Bats jinked above him in the mauve dark. The dog woofed again. He swallowed.

When he was younger he'd been scared of city dogs, Rottweilers and bull terriers, flea-bitten Alsatians howling on flat roofs or behind wire fences. His mam had been bitten by a dog once and wouldn't have one in the house. Not that there were many left since the DARP, only the strays who had managed to avoid being shot.

The yelp fluttered to a stop, one short woof before it gave up. He wondered how a pet dog had survived the cull.

The light went out and he heard someone lock the door. They had forgotten to shut the window, or had deliberately left it to let a cool breeze in. No one did that in the city. Too scared of people getting in and stealing stuff. Unless they had bars. His friend Joe's house had had bars and padlocks. When they were little he and Joe pretended they were in a castle and had sword-fights like the Three Musketeers – Joe's favourite book.

There was no moon, clouds hid the stars. He lifted the window latch carefully and pulled it open wide enough so he could climb in, lowering the backpack in first. The room smelled of wallflowers. He put one foot in front of the next carefully, negotiating the furniture without bumping into it. There was a narrow hallway with doors off it. The kitchen door was open wide. He went straight to the fridge. As he opened it, light flooded the small room, and he closed the door quickly. The fridge hummed and juddered. He shut the kitchen door very quietly and went back to the fridge. Soy milk! He gulped some from the carton. Something meaty and cold sat in a bowl with a plate on it. He stuck his finger into it and sucked. Somehow, without thinking, he had eaten it all and found himself replacing the empty bowl in the fridge. He took a couple of packets of Labmeat and a chunk of cheese substitute. He didn't like cheese substitute, but so what? It's good for you, Mam had said, good for growing bones. He tried to squeeze two tins of baked beans in to the backpack, but couldn't. Why hadn't he left Lo's boots somewhere on the way? He dumped the blanket on the table. Now there was plenty of room. He packed salt, beans, cheese substitute, a bottle of squash, the Labmeat and a box of matches. An unopened carton of dried soy milk caught his eye. Better have that for Lo's growing bones.

The bag was still overfull, so he regretfully replaced the squash. It was stealing to take anything other than food, he reasoned, but guiltily opened a drawer and removed a small sharp kitchen knife and a ball of string and put them into his bag. His eyes fixed on a biscuit tin next to a kettle. His mouth watered. The lid was stiff. He yanked it and it flew off, spinning across the worktop and crashing to the floor.

The dog barked hysterically. A light showed under a door. Loud voices, a man and a woman. He had meant to leave a note apologising for taking the food but explaining that he and his little sister were starving. Now he couldn't. He had to get out. Part of him wanted to give himself up, beg them to look after him and Lo, but he was scared. They might turn them in to the TA. Grabbing a handful of biscuits and the heavy backpack he made for the window. He plucked a pair of sunglasses from the table, put them on, then threw himself out, catching the strap of the backpack on the window stay. Wrenching it free, he tore a hole in his baggies. A man yelled – 'Oi, what do you think you're doing?'

Sid crossed the garden and scaled the wall, shouts and the terrier's excited yelps following him. His heart hammered in his chest. He shivered.

He could be shot.

He could be dead.

Lo could be left all alone, and without him she would not survive.

He ran for what seemed like miles, his legs shaking. But no one seemed to have followed him beyond the garden perimeter. Perhaps they had been scared, too. He stopped and checked that he still had his and Lo's IDs and ran on through the darkness, laughing in fear and triumph. The blanket – he thought – fair exchange for sunglasses and a knife.

CHAPTER FIVE

LO WOKE IN the dark. A slight breeze wafting through the tunnel made a noise like a moaning child. She tried the torch but it was dead.

'You bad girl,' she scolded Rosebud. Her voice sounded loud and echoing. She closed her eyes against the dark and loneliness and cried quietly. Lying down again she scratched her head and clutched her doll.

A small pregnant tabby cat crept into the tunnel, sniffed at the sleeping child, curled its lips at the fossilised fox shit, and after a perfunctory wash lay down and fell asleep close to the sleeping child, ears pricked, ever on the alert. After an hour the cat woke hungry, hunted and ate a mouse, scraped a hollow, shat, covered it and went back to the cave-like pipe, sniffed again at the fox spoor and the sleeping child and curled up on herself.

Lo woke from a dream of her mother calling her.

'Mammy,' she said as she sat up.

Sid was standing over her.

'Watcha, Lo-lo, I've got food.' He lifted the heavy backpack triumphantly.

She rubbed her eyes. 'I want a poo.'

'Outside then, don't do it in the den.'

He led her out into the cool dawn. Birds sang. He took her away from the den and dug a hole with his hands and the poker in the leafy earth. 'Cover it up when you've done,' he said. 'Here's some big leaves to wipe your bum.'

She giggled. 'They're not leaves, they're plates.'

Sid waited at a distance until she was finished, reminded her about kicking the leaves to cover the mess and led her back to the den. He wished he'd taken the spade from the shed. Perhaps he'd go back for it. He thought how their mam had always made them wash their hands and felt guilty that they hadn't been able to do that for ages. He should get a washing supply from the lake. Yeah, he'd do that. Hygiene, that was the word, hygiene. *Now wash your hands*. He'd take the bucket back to the lake and fill it.

'Did you get my wellies, Sid?'

'Yeah, found them. How's your feet?'

She said listlessly, 'I'm hungry.'

They feasted on cheese substitute and water biscuits on a cabbage-leaf plate. Lo wouldn't eat anything green. But she gave hers to the pale blue knitted rabbit, which she clutched as if it would hop away if she put it down. It had one black stitched eye, a small black mouth and a pair of floppy pink ears. It looked sad. 'Don't you like gweens?' she asked it. 'Lo don't like gweens, too.'

Sid tore off a piece of cabbage and chewed it until all the juice had gone then spat it out. They tried to bite into the raw potatoes but they were too hard and tasted awful. So he juggled them instead and made her laugh. It was a long time since they had laughed. He remembered making potato prints at his first school, carving a shape on the cut surface and dipping it in paint.

He pretended to take a potato from Lo's ear. She giggled. When he was seven, he had taught himself magic tricks, because Isambard Kingdom Brunel had performed them for his three children. He imagined the famous man chain-smoking cigars while producing rabbits from his tall black hat. He knew everything there was to know about IKB. Brunel smoked forty cigars a day and died aged fifty-three. Amazing he'd lasted that long, thought Sid. Sometimes he'd thought he'd like to be a magician as well as an engineer. Not much hope of doing either of those things now, he thought, bitterly.

'Thank you for my wabbit, Sid.' Lo lifted her dirty face to her big brother's and kissed his cheek. He smiled and touched her face.

At the swimming pool, as Lo called it, they washed, and Sid swilled out his mouth in a vain attempt to clean his mossy teeth.

'Boat ride, boat ride, boat ride,' she chanted.

'Shh, all right. But you've got to be quiet. Pretend you can't talk. It's like a game, we're both dumb.'

'Dumb?'

'Can't talk.'

She put her hands over her mouth to stop herself talking, and giggled. Invisible birds chirruped and whistled from the trees. Fish rose and kissed the surface of the water and insects with rainbow-coloured wings hovered in the warm air. A breeze whispered in the reeds.

'Don't do that, stupid. You need both hands to get into the boat, don't you?'

'I'm not stupid, and you're a pooey-face.' She frowned at him but did as she was asked and tucked the hem of her fairyprincessdress into her frilly pants to keep it from getting wet. They drifted across the lake, sun flickering through the overhanging trees on their upturned faces.

After he had filled up the containers they trudged back to the den. Lo had wanted to stay by the pool all day, but Sid felt uneasy there. If anyone saw them they wouldn't be able to escape. They would be like flightless ducks. They would be caught and Lo would be taken away.

'Our roundabout den's best. It's safe there. Our secret place.'

'Yeah, secret place.' Lo sucked her thumb and tripped over her boots. 'My feet hurt.' She sat and pulled at her wellies.

'You'll have to carry them, I'm not.' Sid was sweating from carrying the water.

'Don't care.' But she soon got a splinter in her foot and yelled out.

He put down the containers. 'Shh, don't make so much noise, Lo.' He couldn't get at it with his dirty, bitten-down nails. His mam would have used a needle cleaned in a flame to dig out a splinter. There were so many things you needed to know to look after a small child. He sighed. 'Put yer boots back on, Lo, it won't hurt so much.'

Inevitably he ended up carrying her on his back, the bag over his shoulder, the water sloshing over the side of the bucket. She kept up a low whimper all the way back. The occasional rumble of a heavy vehicle reached them, but they saw no one.

The cat had made a shallow nest in the leafy bed of the den. Her time was near, and she had decided this was the safest place, but she slunk away at the sound of the children returning and waited until they slept before sneaking back.

CHAPTER SIX

THE BIKERS CAME again that night. Twenty of them. They came from the direction of Hayle, roared and raced around the roundabout, then disappeared along the A-road to the next town.

Except for one. The last rider. He was leaning over too far, his Harley Davidson skidded and spun away from him and he rolled over and over and landed in the middle of brambles on the roundabout.

Sid woke. He heard the rest of the riders as they carried on with their journey, unaware of what had happened. He listened to the silence that followed.

He crept to the edge of the roundabout and looked at the crashed bike. No rider to be seen. He must be on the other side of the bike, he thought. There was no other traffic; no army trucks, no tanks. He ran out to the mangled Harley. No one there. Where was the rider? He looked about the road, but couldn't see a body. The man must have got up and walked away.

They went to the lake again. Sid found another way to it, well away from the mushroom field. It was a longer journey, but he didn't want to bump into any foragers. They swam and bathed and rowed.

'Mammy would like it here,' Lo said. 'Show me the photo.' She stared at the stained paper. 'Is that her?'

'Yeah, course it is, stupid.'

'I'm not stupid and you're a pooey-face. Where's Dad's wheelie-chair?'

'It's a photo of their wedding day, isn't it? Before the accident. When Dad had legs to stand on.'

'I like him in his wheelie chair,' she whispered.

They trekked back through the wood, and Sid picked up the spade and rope from the derelict building. They listened at the road and crossed to the roundabout.

'What's that funny noise, Sid?'

'Shh!' They stood still and listened.

A moan. Not the moan of wind blowing through the tunnel. Another sort of moan.

It was difficult dragging the injured man out of the brambles. He was heavy, big. Sid was scared of injuring him more. The biker's leathers were torn and bloody, his helmet still strapped under his chin, the visor hiding his face, an angel design on the helmet, a white angel, and on the back of his black jacket was the design of white wings.

'Is it an angel? Did he fall out the sky?'

'Shh, he's hurt bad. Gimme the water.'

'Will he eat all our food? Will he help us find Mammy and Dadda? Will he fly away when he's better? Is he dead?

The next day an army truck came and two TA soldiers removed the wrecked motorbike.

'Fancy walking away from that! Lucky bugger, eh!'

A bulky, broad, strong man. Big hands. White lines splayed out from grey eyes. A tattooed angel on his bald head. Hairy nostrils and ears that reminded Sid of Gramps. The grandfather he was hoping to find in the Far West. He and Gramps had looked over a bridge at quivering trout. Before Lo was born. Before everything started to go wrong.

Sid held his water bottle to the man's parched lips. He gulped at it, water spilling over his gingery beard and onto his chest.

'You're injured,' said Sid. 'What's your name?'

'Call me Mal,' the man croaked.

Sid offered his hand as he had seen his father do with strangers. 'I'm Sid.'

The man tried to lift his right arm and failed.

'Thanks, Sid. I owe you. Er, was there a pannier?'

'A what?'

'A bag attached to the bike?'

'Dunno. The soldiers must have found it.'

The lie made Sid's cheeks redden. He had looked inside the pannier, with some guilt. It was private, he shouldn't have, but somehow privacy and things like that had all disappeared with The Emergency. There might have been food or something they could have used. He had hidden the rifle under a log, far from the den, and made sure that Lo hadn't seen. There was ammunition too. The first-aid kit was brilliant; he wouldn't have managed to help the man without it. There were scissors, needles and cotton, a big torch, batteries, rope. A huge haul. But no food.

Lo fed the man a few beans from the tin.

'Are you an angel?'

'Yeah.' He tried to grin but it hurt. Everything hurt.

She danced around twirling her tatty skirt.

'An angel, an angel! Do all angels eat beans? Where's your wings?'

He tried to get up but could not. He swore.

'That's a naughty word,' Lo scolded.

Sid held his head and got him to sip more water, then laid him down gently. Where his leathers were torn his hip and thigh were exposed and the tattooed words

God, where are you?

Sid was in a terrible quandary. He knew who the man was. He should have killed him, not saved his life. But killing was wrong. He was thinking ahead, of what to do when the man was well enough to walk. He had a plan.

CHAPTER SEVEN

HE HAD NO MEMORY of the accident or anything that had happened that day. He was perplexed at how he had got here in this tunnel and why these children were caring for him. He vaguely remembered being at the depot and getting into his leathers.

Every time he closed his eyes the nightmare descended, except that it wasn't a nightmare, it was true. His first job. He saw her blue eyes as they had dimmed.

This little girl looked very like her – same skinny limbs, hollow cheeks, dark smudges under her eyes, messy pale hair. He sank into himself again, pain pushing him into unconsciousness, a place he was keen to stay away from.

'I don't like the noises he makes,' Lo complained.

'He's only dreaming, Lo. A bad dream. About coming off his bike, I expect.'

'It frightens me,' she hiccupped.

After Sid cleaned and covered the hip wound with an antiseptic dressing the man had sunk into a deep slumber.

Sid smeared the biker's ointment on Lo's festering blisters and stuck plasters over them, and on the scratches on her arms. She was delighted with them, as proud as if they had been medals. He put a small round plaster on his own sore heel, too.

'I hurt myself bad, didn't I, Sid? Bad as the angel?'

With the sewing kit he mended the hole in his baggies. Pricked himself a dozen times but he'd done it. Proud of himself, he was. Wished his mam could have seen him.

There were no more baked beans or Labmeat and the milk powder was nearly used up. All they had now was water and dried soup powder. Sid had no choice. He would have to leave Lo with the injured man and hunt for more food. Her 'angel' was immobile, for the time being, but to make sure, Sid tied him up and blindfolded him. The man was unconscious again, but he wasn't going to take any chances.

'What yer doing that for, Sid?' Lo was upset. He took her on his lap and jogged her up and down. She wiped her nose on her arm.

'We don't want him to know where our secret den is, do we? I won't be long. Promise. Stay here. Don't move. You can guard him, eh? Give him water if he wants?'

She nodded, reluctantly.

'You'll be okay, yeah? Won't be long.'

With the empty backpack flapping on his naked back, Sid jogged through fields he knew from his other sorties, keeping a careful eye open for danger.

Wild ducks waddled through the meadow, stretching their necks to sip at the seed heads of grasses. It gave him an idea.

Avoiding the farmer with horse and plough and the bending labourers in the dusty fields, he kept an eye open for the armed guard, and made for the uncut edge of a field of corn. He plucked a ripe yellow head and chomped on it, spitting out the chaff and nibbling the nutty grain. It was good, like raw rice but softer. He found more, but it wasn't enough to satisfy his hunger. He was always hungry. It was as if a gnawing worm was inside his empty stomach, never letting him be.

He couldn't risk begging food from the labourers. For Lo's sake, he had to keep his head down.

Be invisible.

He gathered more corn and stuffed it in his pocket. He wore the knife in his belt, like a dagger, dark glasses shaded his eyes; in his imagination he became a desperado, a hunter. Even though he had his ID he avoided people, not wanting to answer awkward questions.

He thought about the man. He remembered the awful words he'd heard from the girl with the dark eyes. 'Population Reduction Programme'. Dad should have listened to Mam. They should have left for the Far West, away from the ghetto. But Dad, stubborn as ever, wanted to stay put.

Big mistake, thought Sid. He wished he hadn't saved the Reducer's life. It was going to be a problem, getting rid of him without him knowing the whereabouts of the den. Perhaps they should abandon the roundabout and run?

'Angel, are you going to stay and look after us?'

'Have to get back to work, don't I?' The pain from his sore shoulder and damaged hip bothered him; the rope around his wrists and ankles was an irritation and he was desperate for a piss.

'What work do angels do? Looking after people?'

'Something like that.'

'Would you like a cuppatea?'

Lo put a leaf to his mouth and stroked his arm. He flinched.

CHAPTER EIGHT

AS SID WENT further away from the roundabout, he noticed new planting on the roadside verges. The labels said – *runner beans, carrots, blackcurrants*. There were fruit bushes covered in black nets. He kept to no-man's land between the verges and the fields, narrow paths of untouched earth where nettles and thistles grew, butterflies fluttered and birds foraged. Everywhere he looked there was planting going on. Women of about his grandparents' age bent and dug, threw seed and stamped it in. Two large horses pulled a plough; gulls and crows rose and fell behind it, black and white, black and white. Hosepipes lay along the fields and water trickled and sprinkled onto the furrows. He bent to drink. The sun burnt the faces of the workers. It had already bleached Sid's light brown hair white. His legs were covered in scratches and gashes, scabs and stings. A bird was singing, he didn't know what it was, but it made him suddenly glad to be alive. He took a deep breath of salty air.

He came across an old stone road sign. Marazion (*Marghas Yow*) five miles. A town with 'z' in it. Was this where his grandparents lived? Five miles wasn't far. He and Lo had walked much further than that, most days on the flight from the city, but he couldn't go today. Food was uppermost in his mind, that and what to do about the Reducer. He had rehidden the rifle and the ammunition a long way from the den, in a burrow in the earth that could have been made by an animal. He had covered it over with a few dead branches and marked a tree nearby with his knife, so he would find it again. Holding the heavy weapon made him feel like a man. But would he be able to use it if he had to? He didn't know why he had wanted to save the Reducer. Except that it is what his father would have done, regardless of who the man was.

The badger, who had given birth to two cubs in the underground chamber a few days before, short-sightedly examined the metal objects at the entrance to her sett, and crept out to find food. She lifted her striped head and sniffed. A pungent smell – Man. She kept well away from the tunnel, waddled across the empty road and dug under a hedge where there was a wasp nest.

CHAPTER NINE

MAL COULDN'T GET UP, couldn't see, bloody kid had blindfolded him too; couldn't free himself. Hurt all over. He felt the presence of the small girl, smelled her close by, heard her snivelling.

'I wish I had my bag of stuff. I've got sweeties in there,' he said, quietly. There was a brief silence. Then...

'Sweeties! I like sweeties.'

'Untie me, girlie, and I'll get the sweeties for you.'

'Lo, Lo, what are you doing?' Sid came through the bushes. I told you to stay in the den.' Sid looked angry, but Lo was too excited to notice.

'The angel has sweeties in his bag, Sid.'

'But you don't have a bag, do you? I told you, the soldiers took it with the bike'. Sid spat the words into the man's face.

'We were going to look for it,' Lo said.

'Oh yeah?' Sid removed the blindfold and Mal blinked.

'You're Runners, aren't you? Is that what you're afraid of? That I'll turn you in?'

'I'm fourteen,' Sid said, defensively.

'But she's under eight, isn't she?' He nodded at Lo, who had wandered off a little way and was kicking at the dry leaf litter. A sycamore key twirled down from its tree and landed at her feet. She picked it up and threw it into the air and watched happily as it spun as it fell.

'What is she? Four, five? And you're hiding her. That's a

punishable offence, these days. Makes you a Runner too.'

Sid remained silent, sorting out the bag of potatoes and greens on the ground.

'But, as I said, I owe you, don't I? Not going to hurt you.' He snorted and spat. 'Potatoes, that's good. Do you know how to cook them?'

Sid shook his head.

'Tell you what, kid – I'll show you how to build an underground fire. That way there'll be no smoke. Undo these, yeah? Dying for a piss. Can't do that for me, eh?' He laughed, a wheezy sound.

Sid imagined the smell of baked potatoes, could almost taste them.

He could see no reason not to undo the ropes. No way could the man get away, the state he was in.

Released from his bonds, went a little way off to relieve himself in the bushes. Sid, picked up the poker, watching him closely. The man took in the situation. The lad wasn't stupid.

'Right kid, got a spade? Good, then dig a pit.'

'Why?'

'Listen, you won't survive unless you eat proper. You want to eat, don't you?'

Sid dug a deepish hole in the earth and under the man's instruction, laid a floor of stones and pebbles. Lo sat nearby, hiccupping and scratching her head. 'I want sweeties,' she whispered to herself.

'Now find some small stuff – dry moss, lichens, twigs.'

Sid carefully built a fire with leaves and moss, then twigs, and finally, dead wood on the top. He put a match to the kindling and they sat round watching the little flames and listening to the comforting sound of crackling wood.

'Wait a while, till there's ashes,' Mal said.

Gathered round the firepit they could have been a family, not illegal Runners and a Reducer whose job it was to kill them. 'Now cover some of the ash with the potatoes and put the rest of the ash on top.' The man tried to raise an arm to help, but groaned and gave up. Sid did as he said.

'Now bury the lot with earth. Bury the lot. It'll take time, but it'll cook them, you'll see.'

'I want sweeties.' Lo curled up and sucked her thumb, trying to keep her eyes open.

'Where you heading?' Mal asked Sid. 'Can't stay here forever, can you?' He hoisted himself over to the tunnel and sat against it, sweating from the pain.

'Why not?'

'Someone might see you; find you. What would you do then? How are you going to protect her?'

Mal nodded at the sleeping girl. The once pink dress was rucked up under her bottom. Sid covered her legs with his T-shirt. The air was cooler now and he shivered.

'Here, have this.' Mal slipped out of the top part of his leathers, moaning at the effort, removed his khaki T-shirt with difficulty and threw it to him.

'Really?'

'Yeah, go on, keep it. Plenty more where that came from.' The man was muscled and spare, with devils tattooed on his hairless chest and a large pair of black wings tattooed across his broad back.

CHAPTER TEN

SID HAD READ the man's identification papers:

REDUCING AGENT 38752, MAL KENT. WEST PENWITH
POPULATION REDUCTION PROGRAM, FORTRESS KERNOW

In scratchy poor handwriting was added:

exterminating angels

When Mal woke in the early hours, as light filtered palely through the trees, he found himself looking up into the barrel of his own loaded rifle.

'What's up kiddo? You don't want to play with that. It could go off and hurt someone.'

Sid's hands shook. He had been awake and watching for hours, trying to decide what to do. His original plan had been to blindfold the Reducer again and lead him far away before releasing him, so that he would have no idea where the den was. But really he should just kill him, make sure he couldn't come back to hunt them down.

After a sleepless night Sid had decided that it would be wiser to do just that, bury him on the roundabout, leave his body to rot, move on with Lo and find his grandparents. But when it came to it, his hands and arms trembled so much he couldn't pull the trigger. Bile rose in his throat and he was close to vomiting.

'Give it me, kid, go on, give it me.' Mal spoke calmly, lifted his good arm and removed the loaded weapon from Sid's sweaty hands. Sid ran off, sobbing with humiliation.

'Brave little bastard,' Mal gave a tombstone grin.

A gunshot woke Lo. She found herself alone and cried, 'Sid, Sid! Where are you, Sid, where are you?'

The Reducer peered into the den. 'It's all right, girlie, he'll be back for breakfast.' She slept again, her skin hot and dry, her breath fetid.

He skinned the rabbit he had shot, groaned with the effort of tearing it to pieces, and buried the pelt and guts, watched by Sid, who hid close by.

Mal searched unsuccessfully for his belongings, all the time spied on by Sid, who would have killed him if he touched Lo. Later Mal limped over to the earth oven, dug up the cooked potatoes and rabbit with his good arm and found the salt. Sid, drawn by the cooking smell, appeared, head down.

'Sid!' Lo hurled herself into his arms.

'Sorry,' he said to the man, as if he had been caught fibbing, not holding a gun to his head.

'Don't worry kid, I won't turn you in. Owe you my life, don't I? Yeah? Told you. Owe you one.'

They ate the meat and hot potatoes, scalding their fingers in the process, but not caring. It reminded Sid of meals long ago, when he'd had a proper home, before The Emergency, before the ghetto.

'Give us the other stuff, yeah? Need my ID. Keep the first aid and torch. I'm leaving.'

'But I want you to stay,' Lo sobbed.

'Angels have work to do. Can't stay here forever, can I?' His red beard bobbed up and down as he spoke. Lo was fascinated. She hugged the tatty toy rabbit to her and sucked her thumb.

'You promise you won't tell anyone about us?' Sid demanded, thin-lipped, trembling.

'Promise.'

Mal held out his good arm to Sid and Sid shook his hand. Mal yanked Sid forward and lightly slapped his face. Sid flinched, before realising that it was a friendly gesture.

'You did good, kid, with the first aid and that. Thanks. You'll be okay.'

'Thanks for the T-shirt,' Sid mumbled. 'Sorry about the gun…' He could feel his face burning.

'No worries, kiddo.'

Lo held up her grubby face to Mal as he said goodbye. He didn't know how to react. No one had ever wanted to kiss him. No child anyway. He bent, embarrassed, and let her peck his cheek, her arms around his neck. He felt the pressure of the little girl's thin arms on his neck and the caress of her chapped lips for a long time.

CHAPTER ELEVEN

THE CAT CREPT into the den again that night. The children slept fitfully, disturbed by thunder and the odd flash of lightning. She gave birth to her litter of three kittens in the dry leaves, licked them clean, polished off the afterbirth and carried them out, one at a time to another hiding place, not far away, but far enough so the children would not hear their small cries.

The owl was aware of the birth, as was the fox. But the cat would not leave her young alone for the meat-hungry creatures to get them. She would guard them fiercely, ready to give up her own life if need be.

Finding their grandparents was now uppermost in his mind. He could remember the road, houses that all looked the same except that theirs had a monkey puzzle tree in the garden. On a hill. What else? An attic window where he looked out at gulls on the roof, asleep facing the wind, buffeted, feathers blown all every way, heads tucked under wings. A stream at the bottom of the road, a humpy stone bridge.

It would be easier if he went on his own; he could go faster. Would Lo survive without him for a couple of days while he trekked to Marazion? If he left her with enough food and water she'd be all right. She seemed to have forgotten Mam and Dad. Hadn't mentioned them for days. Instead, she kept asking about Mal, her angel.

'Why did he leave? I liked him.'

'He wasn't a nice man, Lo.'

'No. He was an angel.'

'Yeah, yeah, an angel,' Sid sighed. He should have killed him. The Reducer wasn't to be trusted. Sid guessed that Mal had grown fond of Lo, but even so, he might tell the authorities about them and someone else would find her and kill her – and him if the Reducer was right.

They were bathing in the lake when a sudden flash of green made Sid look up.

'Look, Lo,' he whispered, 'A kingfisher!'

'What's a kingfisher?' she whispered back, seeing nothing but green trees and darker green water.

It had gone.

'Never mind, we'll see it again.' He was excited. Apart from witnessing the rainbow beauty of the little bird, it reminded him that there were fish in the lake. Maybe he could make a line from the cotton in the Reducer's sewing kit, bend a pin to make a hook, find a worm.

But they needed food now. By the time they got back to the den, Sid had made up his mind. There was nothing for it: he couldn't leave his little sister on her own for long; they would leave the den for now.

He began to pack the things they would need.

'No, Lo, leave it here.' Exasperated, he tried to wrench the soft toy from her, but she held on grimly. 'It'll be safer here. Can look after your dolly, can't he? Till we get back.'

'No! Want Wabbit! Want Wabbit!'

She started to cry.

'Oh, go on then.'

He had packed the first aid kit, torch, batteries, salt and water in his backpack. He also took matches and remains of the food. The knife he slipped into his belt where he could get to it in a hurry. They set off to find the town with a 'z' in it. First he had to find the signpost.

They passed a burnt-out garage, rusty wheel-less cars in the forecourt, and the flimsy shells of burnt-out bungalows, sad with torn flowered wallpaper and the odd shower fittings or washbasin still attached.

'No people,' she remarked.

'No. Nice and quiet, innit?'

A shrieking storm of starlings passed low overhead, startling them.

'Bloody hell, what was that?' he said. They watched in wonder as the flock of thousands snaked across the darkening fields, changing shape like a genie escaped from a lamp.

'My feet hurt,' Lo complained.

'Take your boots off then,' Sid told her. The tarmac was cooling down after a hot day, though a heat haze still shimmered above it. She put the toy rabbit into one of the boots and cuddled it to her.

'Here, give it here.' Sid took the other boot and her sock and squashed them into the bag.

'Can I have a plaster?'

'None left.' He held her hand and they sang as they walked.

'*Hi ho, hi ho, it's off to work we go…*' They didn't know any more words. But the song made them walk quickly and Lo kept hopping and skipping in her bare feet. No traffic passed going either way.

Other roundabouts had only grass, on which foraged oystercatchers, red legs hurrying, red beaks searching. One roundabout had only gravel, on which nothing lived.

'I like *our* roundybout best,' said Lo.

'Yeah, it's the best. We mustn't ever tell anyone about it, right? Our secret.'

'Hold my hand,' said Lo.

'Listen!'

A low rumble. Vibrations under their feet. He ran with her up the bank and into a field of ploughed earth and they kept running until they reached the cover of a low stone hedge. Hiding behind it he watched a convoy of armoured vehicles and troop carriers speed along the road. It took five minutes. Lo had fallen immediately asleep.

'Come on, Lolabelle.' She dragged behind, tugging on his arm like a reluctant dog.

They were just about to go back to the road when another convoy passed and they had to fall flat on their faces onto the soil to avoid detection. He pushed her head down.

'You're hurting me.' She started to cry.

'Shh! It's like a game, Lo, they mustn't see you, okay?'

'Why?'

'Because.'

Instead of getting back onto the main road Sid decided they should head across country. He soon became disoriented and with no sun or moon to guide them he was confused about which way was west.

'Cawwy me, cawwy me,' Lo begged. He did for a while, then put her down. His back ached and he was hot and tired. After what seemed hours, Lo sobbing and dragging on his arm, they seemed to be climbing. As they crossed rough moorland he could see a faint change of light on the horizon – a pale mauve and a dark charcoal line where sea met sky. The sea! He felt confident that they were on the right track and as they scrambled over a stone hedge onto a little road they saw a sign – 'Zennor I mile'. Z! Another town with a 'z' in it!

The moon appeared from behind clouds and lit up a huddle of low cottages, a bridge over a briefly silvered stream.

The heavy door of the old church creaked as he pushed it open. There was a not unpleasant smell of dust and damp and there was the faint glow of moonlight at the coloured glass windows.

'Do angels live here?' Lo asked.

'Hope not.'

Water sat in a granite bowl on a granite plinth. It tasted a bit sour and warm but okay so he filled the bottle from it and they drank. There were leaflets and postcards on a stand. He picked one up to read. He missed books. They gathered together all the small hard embroidered cushions that they found on the wooden benches and made a bed for themselves.

When Sid woke, Lo wasn't there.

'Lo!' he called anxiously.

There were stitched pictures on the hassocks – an angel, a

herring gull, a tractor, a fishing boat, a fish. On one were the words GOD IS LOVE. He found Lo sitting on the angel cushion on a child's chair at a low table in the side chapel, playing at tea parties.

'Lo, there you are.' He thought how he suddenly sounded like his mam.

'Sid, Sid, there's a lady here. Look.' She stood and pointed at a carving on a dark pew end.

'That's a mermaid. Look at her tail,' said Sid.

'Oh, a mermaid!' Lo had once had a book about mermaids.

'There's a story about her. She sang in the choir and a boy fell in love with her.'

'Really?'

'Yes. She took him with her to live in the sea.' He waved the leaflet with the Mermaid of Zennor story in it.

'Did she?' Lo traced the outline of the rough carving with her sticky fingers.

'Not very pretty, is she?' her brother said. '*I* wouldn't jump in the sea for her.'

'Hello, what have we here?' A smiling woman in a blue apron and work boots stood over them. She held a large bunch of dead flowers.

'I'm having a tea party. Do you like my fairyprincessdress?' Lo lifted her trusting face to the woman.

Sid stood between Lo and the stranger. 'I'm Sid,' he said. 'She's my sister Lo and she's eight.'

'Small for eight, isn't she?' The woman laughed pleasantly, not for one moment taken in.

'I'm a big girl,' said Lo.

'Runners, are you?' the woman asked Sid.

'Looking for our grandad, we are. Name of Joe Jenkyn?'

'From around here is he?'

'I think so, yes.'

The woman sniffed. 'Looking for a good bath, I'd say. Have you had breakfast?'

'No,' they chorused.

They followed the woman past a farm gate with a notice that said ORGANIC CATTLE, though there were no cows to be seen, heard or smelt. Sid remembered a lesson at school about it: the culling of cattle and sheep to help stop global warming. They burped too much, or something. Too much CO_2, or was it methane? The woman threw the dead flowers onto a sweet-smelling compost heap. They passed empty barns and sheds, which Sid thought would make great dens, and then he heard the strangest sound. It sounded like a monster groaning. Lo clung to him.

'What's that?' he asked.

'That's Buttercup. Our milk cow.'

'Are you allowed?' Sid asked.

'Oh yes, we have a milk licence. Not all the cows have gone, thank goodness.'

'Will it kill me? asked Lo.

The woman laughed and picked up the small girl and showed her to the cow. Lo giggled, her hand over her mouth. 'It's got eyelashes, like me,' she said.

The woman led them along a sloping mud path with stone hedges on either side. Lo skipped ahead. Dwarf citrus trees had puddles of fallen petals beneath them.

'Look Sid, pink snow.'

Eventually they came to a low cottage by a stream.

'Any fish?' Sid asked hopefully. In the distance he could hear the whispering sea.

'Not enough, my boy. Go in, go on.'

Lo didn't hesitate and Sid followed. It was a small cottage with the front door opening straight into the living room. On a scrubbed pine table was a jug of honeysuckle. A wood-burning stove stood in the fireplace and from it came the smell of bread. The woman told them to wash their hands and sit at the table. Gladly, they did as they were told, marvelling at the clean red checked tablecloth, the brightly coloured rag rug under their feet. Soon they were tucking into warm milk and hunks of freshly baked bread spread with melted butter and blackberry jam.

'Where have you come from?' the woman asked Sid. Before he could answer, the door opened and a man came in. He was tall, with thick dark hair and sad blue eyes.

'Runners?' he asked gruffly.

'They're children in need of food and love, that's all I know.'

'Better get rid of them in the next five minutes, or they'll get more than food and love.'

'What do you mean, Henry?'

'TA's down the lane. We're next on their list, I reckon.'

They bundled the children out of the back door, Lo complaining that she didn't want to go anywhere, Sid trying to remain in control of his emotions.

'Keep on down that path to the beach. They won't go there. Can't get the vehicles down there and too idle to walk.'

Sid prayed she was right. 'Thanks for the food, missus,' he said, a chunk of buttered bread in one hand as he led Lo away. As they hurried off down the coast path they heard the muted rumble of an armoured vehicle.

CHAPTER TWELVE

THERE WERE NO ROLLS of razor-wire or other barricades across the small beach. No coastguards or lookout towers on the looming jagged cliffs. The authorities obviously weren't expecting refugees to attempt landing a boat there. Weed-wreathed rocks punctuated the pebble beach and the sea boiled with white water.

'Is this the seaside?' Lo clung to Sid, alarmed and overwhelmed by the limitless sea. To the small girl it looked like the sea was too high and would inevitably tumble on top of them. They huddled on pebbles against the cliff and watched the waves roll and roll and never stop. Lo picked up the smallest round grey pebbles and put them in Sid's bag. He was contemplating what to do. The sea's never-ending movement was hypnotic. Calming. They sat and stared. After about an hour, they started back along the path to the hamlet. The armoured vehicle had gone. Climbing the few steps into the churchyard they looked at names on the gravestones. Sid examined them all. No Jenkyns. Many graves were new, with fresh flowers in jam jars on them.

'*James and Charlotte Simms. Forever young,*' he read. '*Josephine Kellerman, aged 36 months. Our little angel.*' There were many more, some for entire families, with the inscription '*Sacrificed for the survival of Humanity*'. And he drew Lo away from them as if he feared that she might stay with these little ghosts. They gazed longingly at the cottage where they'd been given bread and jam but there was no sign of the woman.

'Can't we go back to the cow lady?' Lo beseeched.

'No.'

'Why?'

'Because.'

He carried her for a little while on his back before putting her down again. His shoulders were sore.

'How will Mammy find us, Sid?'

'Look at the daisies, aren't they pretty?' Sid was following the little road westwards. He had remembered the name of the other place with 'z' in it. They stopped every now and then to listen carefully for the sound of a vehicle. None came.

'My feet hurt.' Lo whined.

'Look at the seagulls, Lo. Showing us the way, they are.'

A pair of magpies hopped onto the road in front of them, and pecked at a dead badger. Something big had run it over, some time ago. Sid had never seen a badger and thought it was a dog. He picked up Lo and hid her eyes from the dead thing. The magpies reluctantly abandoned the carcass until the children had gone by, then went back to their feast.

'Want to see, want to see,' said Lo.

'No, you don't.'

At the signpost to Marazion they turned off the road and headed along a dusty lane. In the distance were women, heads bent, bundles of straw and twigs on their shoulders, walking the edge of a field. Sid pushed Lo into a dry ditch and put a hand over her mouth. She giggled and squirmed. A robin chipped out an alarm call. When Sid thought it was safe they carried on. A tank churned up the grit on the road they had left. It had a particular sound, louder, slower, but more terrifying than other military vehicles. Even though he couldn't see it, Sid imagined the gun, turning like an alien nose, sniffing them out.

'Cawwy me, cawwy me.'

'Can't always carry you, Lo. Heavy bag. Put on your boots again for a while.'

She grumbled quietly, moaning and sniffing, but did as he suggested. It was quite dark now and there was a full moon.

It was further than he thought. Maybe they should find

somewhere to sleep for the night and carry on early in the morning? They drank from the bottle before moving on. Then in a gap between trees he saw the island, lit by the moon. It looked closer than he remembered. But it was the same island.

'Look Lo, a castle on an island.' The small child gazed at the blue vision, the swathe of light glimmering on the water.

'Look, Wabbit, a faiwy castle,' she whispered.

They came to a large pond with a mass of reeds. The starling flock had only recently roosted and their murmuring rose from the reeds like fluting music. Even Sid was entranced. They carried on and arrived at a pebble beach and they picked up stones and threw them over the rolls of razor-wire into the calm sea.

They made for a disused car park, walked between the tall and untidy buddleia and rosebay willow herb that had grown through the cracks in the old tarmac, and tried the door of a small shed. But it fell off its rusty hinges and a horrible smell came from inside as if someone or something had died in there. Sid dragged her away from it. They walked on, footsore and hungry. There were three old train carriages in a siding. They climbed in through the glassless window of the nearest one and slept on the rotting seats.

Next morning before dawn Sid left Lo sleeping and went to look at the town of Marazion. He was having second thoughts about this place. He could see no terraces of houses with gardens at the front. No monkey puzzle tree. Beyond the rolls of razor-wire on the beaches, were coastguard lookout huts on stilts. The island was much nearer than it should be. They were in the wrong town.

Lo wasn't in the carriage.

'Lo, where are you?' He thought maybe she had woken and gone outside for a wee. The toy rabbit was on the floor under the seat. Lo was nowhere to be seen. In desperation he shouted her name again. No answer.

As he was making a frantic search outside, a skinny man, naked except for a pair of sagging Y-fronts, staggered out of one of the other train coaches. Sid felt for his knife.

'Whassamatter, mate? Lost something?' He had one eye covered in a dirty pink patch, many missing teeth, a long twisted nose with a stud in the side and a grey straggly beard.

A Runner, thought Sid, must be.

The man tried to smile but only achieved an even more fearsome expression. His one eye was yellow and bloodshot.

'My little sister. Eight. Small for her age. You seen her? Pink dress.'

'Might 'ave.' The man didn't look at Sid but focused on a point above his shoulder.

Sid didn't trust him. He could have taken Lo, hidden her in his carriage. He drew out his knife and pointed it at the man. 'Where is she? I'll kill you if you don't let her go.'

'Hold yer horses,' the man laughed, showing black stumps of teeth. 'I ain't got her. Have a look if you don't believe me.' He held the carriage door open. His fingernails were curved claws, filthy and jagged. As he brushed past, the unwashed stink made Sid feel sick.

It was dark inside. The door slammed behind him.

Sid turned, too late.

He found the window, which seemed to be painted on the outside because he couldn't see out of it. He yanked at it but it would not shift. He shouted, but knew it was useless, he was trapped. As his eyes grew accustomed to the gloom he saw that it was an old sleeping carriage with two bunk beds. There were piles of filthy clothes, empty tins, a full water bottle. He wiped the lip with his T-shirt and drank half. Then he banged on the sides of the coach in frustration. In the corner was a cabinet with a wash-basin – no water came from the tap – and underneath was a cupboard, hinged at the bottom and inside was a stained pot. He shat in it, wiped himself on one of the man's vests, which he threw in the pot, replaced it in the cupboard and closed the tilting door. 'That'll teach him, the old sod,' he said to himself.

CHAPTER THIRTEEN

THE PIRATE – THAT'S how Sid thought of him – came back to the sleeping coach after dark, after Sid had heard the starlings again, swarming like bees and screeching above him before they disappeared into the reeds.

'Give us the knife, boy, and you can go.' The man sounded sly.

'No.'

'I'll get it off you anyway. Give it me and I'll let you go.'

'Tell me what happened to my sister.'

'Why should I?'

'Because. Because she's only a baby.'

His voice broke as he said the word baby. She *was* just a baby and he had failed to take care of her. He listened at the door.

Silence.

Then, as if the man thought it was a reasonable argument, he said, 'They took her.'

'Who? Where?'

'How should I know? Women. Three of them.'

'Kidnappers?'

'New-Earthers.'

Sid banged on the door The man was not dangerous, he reckoned, only stupid, though that could be dangerous too.

'What's New-Earthers?'

The man opened the door and Sid fell out, astonished at the sudden blue gaze of the moon and the salt smell of sea-air. He flailed around with the knife but felt the man's bony fingers grasp his wrist and wrench the weapon from him.

'Calm down, sonny boy. I only want the blade. Ain't going to do anything to ya. Not that way inclined, am I?' He examined the weapon and swiped the air with it. Sid was mortified at being beaten by this puny, nearly naked man. But he was free, and frantic to find Lo.

'What's New-Earthers?'

'Live in a wood somewhere. Women Runners.' He coughed and spat green phlegm. 'We've quite a few of Runners in these parts. Plenty of places to hide.'

'Will they hurt her?'

'No idea. No idea. No idea.' He pranced around, the blade glinting. Sid was embarrassed. The man had gone doolally, as his dad would have said.

'Which way did they go?'

The man pointed away from the sea and the island towards the landmass, dark and forbidding.

'Do you know someone called Joe?' Sid asked.

'Who? Joe? Don't know no Joe.' The man laughed maniacally. 'Ho, ho, no, no, don't know no Joe!' He was still laughing and dancing around, scything the thick warm air with the knife, as Sid ran away over the bridge, past the whispering reed beds, to a grass roundabout.

There he saw another signpost – 'Penzance 2 miles'. He was tempted to run towards Penzance, *surely* that must be where his grandparents lived. They would be able to find Lo. He was hungry, thirsty, exhausted, and after all, only a boy. But the trail would be cold if he didn't follow it, he should go after Lo now, while he had the right direction in his mind. Their grandparents might be dead or gone away. Reduced. Anyway, he might not be able to find them. Undecided, he ran across the empty main road and eventually onto the high moor. He stumbled towards the treeless hills, the unknown dark mass of granite outcrops, where the wind sighed and nightjars crept, and where a large dog fox caught scent of the frightened boy, and flattened himself to the still warm earth, ears back, teeth bared, until he had passed.

Darkness fell late in the far southwest, but when it came it was solid, heavy, enveloping, and he had to listen to it, smell it, touch it, feel it with all his senses, to become part of the night.

CHAPTER FOURTEEN

SID SLID OVER boulders, caught his clothes on brambles and scratched his face on stunted blackthorn. He needed somewhere to spend the rest of the night. On a hillside he reached a metal gate, tied shut with wire. He climbed over it, his heart beating loudly at the creak it made. Before him was the entrance to a stone-built farmhouse. There was no door, and the wind blew through the lifeless rooms. He crept into a corner like a stray dog and slept fitfully, a torn curtain his only blanket, woken every now and again by gusts of wind rattling the broken sashes and banging the inner doors. On the wind was a smell of gorse flowers and something else, sweet and putrefying.

At dawn, a vixen screeched three times.

They came for her while she was sleeping. A whisper in her ear, a strong arm that whisked her up and out and away. She didn't struggle. In her befuddled mind it was her mam who had come for her.

'Sid says I'm eight,' she told the red-haired woman, in whose arms she found herself.

'Yes, sweetheart, of course you are,' the young woman said in a soft, sing-song voice. She and the other women kept an eye on the skinny man in his underwear, who stared at them with his one eye from the old carriage.

'Are you taking me away?'

'Taking you somewhere safe and lovely. You'll see.'

'Is Sid there?'

As she was carried along, Lo fell asleep again, feeling safe wrapped up in a clean blanket and held in strong arms.

When she woke there was canvas surrounding her, a brisk breeze whining through the gaps. Her mouth and eyes felt dry. She couldn't focus. She slept again, a poor sleep with many dreams of shooting and hurrying and screams. Her skin was hot, dry, fevered.

Someone gave her a warm sweet drink and she slept again.

Lo had cried at first, missing Sid and Wabbit but had been soothed by kisses and goat's milk. As well as a goat there was a pig, several chickens, real rabbits and white ducks. There were other little girls to play with, a stream, even a donkey to ride. She was scared of its large yellow teeth, fascinated by the long silky ears. And women, soft bosomed women, like her mammy. She thought this might be heaven, though she hadn't yet met any angels.

'Is there a monster?' she asked the smiley woman who held her in her arms and introduced her to the goat.

'No monsters, sweetheart.'

Lo plucked at the woman's fine fair hair and sniffed it. Mam had hair this colour too, but it hadn't smelled nice and clean like this did. Sucking her thumb she nuzzled her head into the woman's warm neck.

'Why's it got funny eyes?'

'Has it? I suppose it has. I don't know, sweetheart.'

Lo liked being called sweetheart. 'He's called Billy,' she announced.

'Actually, she's a girl, like you, and she's called Wilhelmina.'

'She's got a beard,' Lo pointed and laughed.

At first light Sid looked around the building in case there was something of use. There was a table with a dirty oilcloth, a wooden chair, a sunken greasy armchair, a bed with a soiled thin mattress and no coverings, and an old cast iron oven, cold as ice. The living room ceiling was yellow-brown, smoke-stained. And in the sooty fireplace, a dead jackdaw, its claws curled tight.

All the windows were broken. The Victorian coloured glass of the entrance porch, red, yellow, deep blue glass, splintered but churchlike, threw coloured lights onto the ceiling and walls.

Sid was angry at a world where beauty was broken for the sake of it.

He became aware of a lark singing hysterically as it rose higher and higher. This wouldn't do, lingering here. There was nothing to take, no weapons, no food. In the yard he drank from a metal trough and filled his bottle. He opened the door to the barn and gagged as he smelled, then saw, the decomposing body of a man hanging from the rafters by a rope. Blue-black flesh melting on his bones, skin peeling off. Sid pressed his T-shirt to his nose and mouth. On the straw-scattered earth nearby was a dog half eaten by rats, its teeth frozen in an eternal snarl. It had been shot. He found a rifle, barely hidden by the kicked-over chair, in straw under the hanging body. The man must have first shot his dog, then tried to shoot himself, but only managed to shoot off an ear and part of his jaw. Then he must have hanged himself.

Searching in the man's jacket, which had been hung on the chair back, Sid found a box of lead shot. He quietly closed the barn door and vomited.

Sid walked fast, glad to put distance between himself and the farm. In the middle of one field, there was a circular stone on a plinth, with a cross carved into the head. Hairy green lichens sprouted from the stone, like whiskers.

There was nothing, not even potatoes growing in the poor soil. He found a horse mushroom that hadn't been too chewed by slugs and ate it hungrily. Hoping for more in the field, he saw the white tip of a rabbit's scut as it leapt away and heard gulls calling to each other as they flew westward. The sea was on both sides of him, the little island on one side and the rocky coast on the other, a very narrow strip of land.

On one side the soil was richer and there were crops, on the other side it was poorer soil, windswept and bleak.

Belatedly, he thought that now he had a rifle he could have shot the rabbit.

From this height Sid could see a big town – it must be Penzance, and just outside the town, a heliport with military helicopters and a lookout tower. Sid had the Reducer's khaki T-shirt to camouflage him and he rubbed mud onto his face in stripes, like a soldier. Skirting fields and keeping low, he moved away from the town, onto the higher moor. A pair of buzzards cried above him, *keow, keow*. White butterflies with orange tips flitted among the heather and gorse. He wanted to lie down in the short grass and pretend to be happy. But he had to go on. He drank from his bottle and chewed a piece of sweet green grass. There was one low thorn tree, bent away from the prevailing wind, contorted and humped like an old witch in a story.

He thought of little Lo, and was terrified at the idea of not finding her. He didn't trust the old one-eyed man. He'd never heard of New-Earthers. Maybe they were a figment of the crazy man's imagination. He might never see Lo again. No, he would never think that.

A bee buzzed in a gorse flower. The buzzing sound grew louder, but it wasn't the bee. Sid dived for cover, flattening himself on the ground as the helicopter roared overhead, not daring to look up until the noise had been replaced by the bee, still looking for pollen. He wished he were a bee or a butterfly, unaware of danger, unaware of sudden death. He lay there for a minute watching a small black spider jump from stone to leaf. He had no idea that spiders could jump. And ants! So many ants, carrying dead sisters and brothers, or maybe mothers and fathers, purposefully, it seemed to him. What were they doing with their small lives? What should he do with his?

He took off his trainers and socks and walked barefoot, savouring the sensation of cool grass between his toes. This is what it's like to live in the country, he thought. When I find Lo, we'll live somewhere like this, where you can hear birdsong and see the sea. He breathed in the clean air and coughed. As the ground cover became thicker and thornier he put on his shoes and made his way towards a distant wooded valley.

The dense wood was full of birdsong but no sign of a camp. He stopped for a moment to watch a squirrel carry a hazel nut and bury it under the layer of leaf mould. Sid trudged out of the wood and up the side of the valley to high ground. The wind moaned between the rocks. There were no trees up here, only stunted blackthorn leaning away from the prevailing south-westerlies. He clambered onto the outcrop of lichen-covered boulders. From this high point he could see the sea on both sides of the narrow peninsular. To the south was the town, three miles or so away, and all around him were moors with granite outcrops. But he could see that there were many wooded valleys and cliffs that edged both coasts. How was he ever going to find Lo?

Clouds gathered, large and fast moving, until they built into anvils, and shed large lumps of hail, flattening thistles and dandelions and soaking him. Lightning lit the darkened sky and thunder crashed immediately overhead. He had never bothered to notice storms in the city, there had been too much other noise, cars hooting, wheels screeching, before The Emergency. And afterwards, when the civilian traffic stopped, he remembered only the sound of guns and people shouting, but here the big sky seemed to be all around him and he felt as though he were being chased by daggers of fire. He ran, the rifle over one shoulder, downhill towards the clumps of trees, leaping over boulders and thickets of thorns. He pretended he was a soldier being shot at by a deadly enemy. He darted from cover to cover, moving speedily, camouflaged. He arrived at the first trees and slowed to get his bearings. Newly sawn branches were propped up obscuring a gate. One had fallen down to reveal a handmade notice: FREEDOM FARM was written in green paint. In smaller letters underneath were the words NO MALES ALLOWED.

Spelling not being Sid's strong subject, he thought male meant letters.

The last time he had received a card was years ago from his Gramps. It said that he was looking forward to seeing him again one day, and they would sail a model boat on a pond and he would take him to see the tall ships. Sid didn't know what tall ships were, but he liked the card, which showed a 3-D image of a man running. You turned it one way and the man stood still and turned it another and the man's legs were running. He wished he still had it. It had been left with all their belongings in the flat at

Brunel Avenue. It felt like a hundred years ago.

He heard the laughter of girls and thought he must be dreaming. He hid behind a tree as three young women ran by, chasing each other. They wore a sort of uniform and carried baskets. One of them caught the sleeve of another, who dropped her basket and shouted in mock fury at her attacker. They went back to retrieve the nuts that had scattered.

Sid held his breath, not wanting to give himself away. Who were they? Were these the New-Earthers? It didn't seem likely that they had kidnapped Lo. They were dressed in pale green T-shirts and shorts and were barefoot. In the dark bedraggled hair of the youngest, who could have been fifteen, was a daisy chain, little white and yellow stars around her head. He had never seen anyone or anything more beautiful. They ran off into the woods, baskets on their arms, still relaxed and playing as if they had no cares in the world.

He waited until they had disappeared before collecting the nuts that had been missed. They looked a little like acorns, but flatter and with a papery leaf crown. He cracked them in his teeth and ate them. As he followed the girls, his rifle broken and held over his arm, he soon realised that most of the trees were nut trees. There were other trees with fruit dripping from them. He recognised apples and pears and the pale trunks of olives. Others were strange to him. He was surrounded by food. The sunglasses slid down his nose.

Lo had been bathed in rainwater, her hair scrubbed, cut short and combed with herbs to remove head lice. She wore green shorts and T-shirt and her feet were bare. They had promised she could have her pink dress back soon, when it had been deloused. But now she had to learn to be a Forest Fairy.

'A forest fairy?' It sounded good. She wanted to be a Forest Fairy like the other little girls. Their names were Sweetpea and Sand.

'I want my wellie boots.'

'It's nice to go barefoot, you'll see.'

'I have a splinter.'

The smiley lady removed the splinter with a clean needle. She picked at the dry skin, carefully, keeping the little girl occupied by singing a song to her and getting her to join in.

'*If you go down to the woods today…*' she sang, and eventually got the tiny fragment out. Lo only flinched once. Sid would have been proud of her.

'We're going to give you a new name,' the woman whose name she learned was Storm told her.

'But I have a name. My name is Lolabelle Maeve Freeman and I live at 22 Brunel Avenue.'

'Well, Lolabelle, that's a very pretty name, but in Freedom we all get to have new names. We shall choose yours tomorrow.'

'Why must I have a new name?' Lo began to whimper and sucked her thumb, longing for Wabbit or Sid to comfort her.

Storm, who had grey hair, a thin red nose and cold fingers, clicked her tongue and turned away. 'See to her, will you, Moth?' The smiley woman scooped Lo up and swung her around in her plump arms, whooping and laughing.

'My little darling, you'll be happy here, believe me. We have apples and water and lovely tents. It's safe here. It's like a holiday camp.' Lo had never been called a little darling, though Mammy had sometimes called her Sweetpea. And she had never been on holiday.

'But I don't want another name. Want my own name. Want my pink dwess. Want Sid.' She sobbed onto the soft warm breast of Moth, who soothed her and patted her hair.

Presently Lo announced, 'I want my new name to be called. Little Darling.'

Moth laughed and said, 'We'll see.' Lo knew what that meant. It meant no.

'Moff,' Lo whispered to herself, 'Moff.'

CHAPTER FIFTEEN

IN A CLEARING stood a large yurt and several old caravans, hidden from above by a canopy of evergreens. Sid stayed hidden behind a tree and watched as the three girls went into one of the vans. He couldn't take his eyes off the daisy girl.

He stood there for ten minutes. A skinny old woman came out of the yurt and hurried off to one of the vans. He could smell fresh bread baking. His mouth watered. There were chickens clucking among the trees, scraping the loose leafy earth with their yellow claws, red combs flopping over their faces as they pecked and searched. It would be easy to pick one up and strangle it. He could make a firepit and cook it.

Two of the girls came out of the van, but not his girl. They were giggling and holding hands. He crept to the van, and keeping down, moved to the window. There was a wooden bench. He stood on it and peeped in through red check curtains. At first he saw nothing, then he saw her. She was washing her hair over an enamel basin, pouring a jug of water over her head. She wore a towel around her shoulders. He was mesmerised. Her hair looked like a black stream, or the glossy feathers of a rook. His heart leaped under his ribs.

'Oi, what do you think you are doing?'

He practically fell off the bench. It was a small square woman, a red stain masking the left half of her face. Her hands were on her hips.

He tried to run away but she grabbed his arm and although he twisted and wriggled furiously, she held tight.

'No males allowed in here. Can't you read?'

'Let me go then.'

'Is that loaded?'

'Yeah.' He was suddenly brave again. Raising the rifle to his shoulder he hit himself in the eye with the stock. 'Ouch!'

'Well, be careful it doesn't go off. It's bigger than you.' She laughed a long belly-laugh.

Embarrassed, he rubbed his eye.

'Have some bread before you go?' Her tone was softer, sympathetic.

'Bread?' He thought she was kidding, torturing him with the idea of fresh bread. His stomach rumbled.

'Go on, you look hungry, son.'

He nodded.

'Come on then.' She let go his arm and waddled off.

Her caravan was slightly apart from the others, with a picket fence around a small garden planted with fruit bushes, salad leaves and flowers.

'Wait here,' she told him and disappeared inside. Sid wondered if it was a trick. Was she going for help? Would he be captured, beaten? He didn't know whether to stay or run. He rubbed his sore eye again. She emerged a moment later with a plate of crusty bread and goat's cheese. He almost fell on it, but remembering his manners, said 'Thanks!' before he shoved it into his mouth, savouring the butter on the bread and the crumbly texture of sharp white cheese. His thoughts were confused. He needed to find Lo and he wanted to see the daisy girl again. He was grateful to this woman, but more than that, he wanted her to hug him, he wanted to pretend that she was his mother. He missed his mother so very much. Tears came suddenly and he got what he wanted – she held him to her, patting his back and shushing his muffled wails. She smelt of bread and clean sweat.

He blew his nose on the rag she gave him and dried his eyes.

When he looked at her face he was surprised to see that she too had brimming eyes. She held him to her and kept saying tearfully,

'There, there. Son, son.' She eventually pushed him from her. 'You better hop it before Storm sees you.'

'Have you seen my little sister? She's called Lolabelle.'

'How old is she?'

'Eight... five. Went missing two days ago. Pink dress, wellies. She's got fair hair.'

'What did you say her name was?'

'Lo. Lolabelle Freeman.'

'Yes, we've got her. She's safe here. What's your name?'

'Sid. They took my mam and dad.' There – he'd said the words, and saying the words made it real. 'Why did you take Lo?' he wailed. 'She's my responsibility. Mam said I must look after her.'

'She's better off here than on the road with you, isn't she? We've got fresh food, clean water. Other little girls for her to play with.'

'Can't I stay too?' he implored.

'No males allowed.'

'Why?'

She shrugged. 'Freedom rules.'

'Can I see her?'

The woman took him by his grubby hand and led him through the wood, via dirt paths edged with shells. She left him hiding behind a water butt, went into a large green and yellow camouflaged tent and came out with Lo. He didn't recognise her at first. She was clean, her hair was short and fluffy and she was dressed in dark green shorts and T-shirt. She was carrying a large white rabbit.

'Lo,' he called, and she ran to him. He drew her behind the barrel. 'You okay?'

'My name's not Lo any more.'

'Whaddyamean?'

'I don't have a new name yet but I'm a Fowest Faiwy. I want my new name to be Little Darling.'

'Do you want to stay here, Lo?'

'They have weal wabbits. He's mine.' She cuddled the rabbit harder. It struggled and its eyes bulged alarmingly but she held on to it.

'Lo, I'm going to find Gramps and then come back for you,

all right? You'll be safe here. See you later, eh?' He sniffed loudly.

'You bin crying?'

'Nah, gotta cold. He kissed the top of her head.

'Be good, be safe,' she said wistfully, and he slipped away into the woods.

At least Lo was being well looked after. Better than if she was still with him, he reckoned. A load had been lifted from his shoulders. He could move about freely now, with no fear of Lo being taken from him by the TA or the Reducers. If the pirate man was right there were more pockets of resistance like Freedom Farm, dotted about in the far west. There were plenty of wooded valleys between the windswept moors and the sea on both sides of the peninsula. Plenty of places to hide. Like the roundabout. And the military hadn't found Freedom Farm. Yet. He was struck by a terrible thought: what if Freedom Farm was raided and Lo was taken? He wouldn't know what had happened to her. He would try to find his grandfather as soon as possible, then go back for Lo.

It wasn't until he was on his way with bread, nuts and apples, and a fresh supply of water in his backpack that it occurred to him that he hadn't asked the kind woman's name and he hadn't found out the name of the daisy girl. He thought about the girl as he trudged over the windswept moor, the slender shape of her, her smile, her bowed head and the waterfall of her wet hair.

He drew closer to Penzance, keeping to the edges of the little fields, taking care not to step on the crops. He saw four farm workers and went towards them. They looked up and seeing that it was only a weedy looking boy, went back to their work. He felt a flicker of anger. They should respect him – he had a rifle hidden under his backpack. As he drew closer to them he saw that they were all women, dressed in dungarees and boots, dark stains under their arms.

'What do you want?'

'I'm looking for my grandfather – Joe Jenkyn?'

'Don't know him,' one said. The others ignored him. He thought how sad and ugly they looked, their mouths down-turned, hair cropped, faces red from the wind and sun.

'Has a monkey puzzle tree in his garden?'

'Better get going,' one said. 'Before the bogey man gets you.' One of them put her arms up in the air and pretended to growl at him. They laughed.

When he got far enough away so they couldn't catch him he aimed the rifle and pulled the trigger. He saw the earth explode close to them, and shattered clods of dirt like a sudden dark fountain. They yelled and shook their fists and he laughed, although horrified at what he'd nearly done, and ran away.

Crossing a couple of wide roads, an old overpass where grass and shrubs were already pushing up between cracks in the tarmac, brown and gold butterflies hovering over them, he looked down on the town and the harbour. A ship lay rusting in the dry dock, and the seawall bristled with spikes and big rolls of razor-wire. Watchtowers dotted the coastline around the bay to Marazion, opposite the island with the castle. The slate roofs were covered in orange lichen, and to his eyes it looked as if a giant had poured orange juice over them. Where he'd come from all the roofs had been painted white to counteract The Warming. Maybe they hadn't heard about it here.

CHAPTER SIXTEEN

THERE WAS A market in a disused car park next to the old railway station and yard. He didn't have to hide any more, now that he hadn't got Lo to look after. But he kept the rifle out of sight, tucked into his backpack and disguised by his blue T-shirt. Scruffy people sat on the ground with produce on cloths in front of them. There were red-skinned potatoes, plump cauliflowers, turnips, great orange pumpkins, bunches of onions and herbs. A vendor cooked skewered onions and peppers on a charcoal griddle. A woman sold pasties from a tray hanging around her neck. Sid's mouth watered at the smells.

'What's in it?' he asked.

'Potato, carrot and swede, what do you think?' she said.

He bought one with the only coins he had and ate it slowly, savouring the pastry, the juicy gravy, the vegetables and herbs. He sucked his fingers and felt almost happy.

A brass band made up of five women and one man was playing in the middle of the road. It was interrupted by a loud siren blaring from a loudspeaker on a pole.

Simultaneously, many of the market shoppers and vendors dropped everything and all ran in the same direction along the sea front, following a man yelling, 'Thief, thief!' They chased after a skinny woman clutching a large cauliflower. Soldiers piled out of an armoured vehicle and bundled her into the back. The dropped cauliflower rolled across the road like a decapitated head and came to a stop in the gutter. The man who been robbed picked it up and blew at it to remove the dirt. The rabble turned back to their market, looking almost disappointed. Sid made no eye contact with anyone. He bypassed the market place and headed for the other end of the town, passing an old swimming pool set next to the sea wall. Next to the entrance there was a sign – Jubilee Pool – and above it – Territorial Army HQ. He could see that the pool was empty of water but filling up with people in uniform. On the road were parked jeeps, just like the one in which he and Lo had been placed after his parents were taken away.

His stomach churned. He turned away from the pool and walked quickly along the road in the opposite direction to the market place.

There were plenty of women on old bikes with baskets on the front. Not many men, he noticed, only ones in uniform. No kids. He felt conspicuous.

His rifle was concealed by his side, the bag over it. A city kid, Sid knew to keep to back-alleys and lanes to avoid crowds. A bold brown rat ran down a flight of granite steps as he climbed up them. He thought how there would be fewer rats if the authorities hadn't killed all the dogs and cats to save energy and food. How the rats had no natural enemies so now they had drains, sewers and rubbish to themselves. Even the huge gulls seemed intimidated by them, leaving the rubbish when a rat attacked.

Soon people would have to eat the rats, he thought, now that meat was scarce, and he wondered why no one had thought of it before. Rat would probably be as tasty as rabbit. Rat pasties. Yuk. Rabbit pasties would be a good idea. Perhaps he could supply rabbits to the pasty maker? He didn't fancy eating gull though – fishy, tough, greasy things, they'd be.

As he came out of a steep lane onto the promenade, he saw huge piles of rusting vehicles acting as a barrier to keep the sea back and presumably to stop refugees getting in. Part of the sea defences. He had seen them used like this before, cars and old tellies and computers, all useless now there was no petrol and no electricity for most people.

Penzance was bigger than he remembered it. But he had been

only four or five when he was here before. A little kid, like Lo. In spite of the awful weather, Gramps had taken him to the beach, but he hadn't gone into the water. The waves were too high and greedy. They would have grabbed him and dragged him under, his Gramps had said. Instead, they had flung pebbles into the sea.

Now he had a firearm and he was on a quest with big responsibilities. Find his grandfather and fetch Lo from Freedom, and then they would live happily ever after. Possibly.

He crossed a small metal bridge over rushing water, rusted ships to either side of it. He found himself by another harbour where a dozen or more fishing boats had been scuttled, sunk and broken like toy boats in a bath. Doors swung creaking on empty sheds that still smelled of fish, even though there had been no fish landed here for many years. Hungry gulls screamed above. There was a small public garden on his right. It hadn't yet been planted with food crops. A deflated football was high and dry in the empty pond. He went in and sat against a wall, facing the lowering sun, the orange and pink washed sky, took out a chunk of bread and chewed it thankfully, thinking of the plump woman with the red-stained face and remembering that she had called him Son. Maybe she had lost her own son? Maybe he had been disappeared, reduced? He curled up on the dry grass, hidden from the road by the low wall, and slept.

He dreamed of a girl with daisies in her hair smiling down at him. She was on a swing and she kept swinging closer and closer to him and then she fell off.

He woke, aching and cold. It was still night-time; gulls called to each other through the dark. He looked in his backpack for his T-shirt and put it on over the khaki one. He wondered what had happened to Mal. Had he taken the Exterminating Angels to look for the roundabout den? Were they still searching for Lo? He shivered and watched the pinpricks of stars and listened to the waves crashing over the harbour wall. His head itched unbearably and he took out the scissors from the first aid kit and hacked at his hair, cutting it as close to his head as he could without hurting himself. He remembered he had some of the Reducer's cash left and wondered if he could find a shop when it was light, for a nit comb, but then thought better of it. Finding Gramps was his priority.

Hours later, a dull grey dawn broke. He was still shivering.

'What yer doin, man?' Green eyes from a narrow, freckled, face regarded him from the wall behind him. He jumped up, trying to look fierce. Had he been robbed in his sleep? He remembered the rifle but fumbling he dropped it.

'Is that real or pretend?'

'Real of course.'

'You're not allowed.'

'Who says?'

'Them. TA.'

'Just try and stop me.'

'What camp are you in?' said the grinning boy.

'Whaddyamean?'

'Aren't you in a Repop camp?'

'Are you?'

'Course I am, man. Newlyn North Camp, me.'

'What do you do there?'

'Stuff. With other kids.'

'Do you know a man called Joe Jenkyn?'

'Nah. What's your name?'

'What's yours?'

'Tell us yours first.'

The boy wore sand-coloured shorts, a T-shirt and a baseball cap with Repop embroidered on it. He had a cotton scarf tied around his neck with an oak leaf motif embroidered in green. He looked well fed and relaxed, not at all scared of the rifle. He turned his cap the wrong way round, briefly revealing his shaved head, and grinned again.

'Sid,' said Sid.

'Mine's Buzz. Short for Buzzard, but I don't like it much.' He jumped down and stood in front of Sid. Sid had never seen anyone with green eyes and white eyelashes before.

'Buzzard?' They giggled together at the ludicrous sounding name and the giggles turned into hysterical laughter.

'Buzzard?'

'Buzzard!' They fell about, slapping each other on the back, falling down and rolling around in the dust. It was Sid's first laugh since he and Lo had run away. He felt empty of emotion, as if he had been drowned and born again.

When they came to their senses they wiped away tears of laughter.

Sid said, 'Want some bread and cheese? It's real.'

Buzz cheerfully took it and stuffed it into his mouth.

'Mm, thanks. Where do you live?' Buzz asked.

'Here and there.'

'You aren't a Runner are you?'

'Nah, I'm fourteen and I'm not sick.'

Words from another Runner came back to him – 'You'll be able to mate and have kids of your own later on, when the world is able to feed a bigger population.' The boy who had told him this was sixteen, and fearful of being caught. 'You're one of the lucky ones, you are. You'll be able to do lots of girls.'

Sid had blushed deeply.

Buzz pulled his cap around the right way and put away the remains of his snack. 'You don't look fourteen.' Buzz was not much shorter than Sid. 'Come meet my mates then.'

Sid picked up his pack and the rifle and followed the boy as he ran up cobbled alleyways and over granite walls, through gardens and back yards and down stone steps.

Sid was desperate to know if Buzz had also lost his parents in the Reduction Programme but shyness or something else – a deep hurt whenever he thought about his parents and Lo – stopped him. Were there camps of kids like him all over? Is that where he would have ended up if he hadn't escaped from the jeep with Lo?

They came at last to a huge church halfway up a hill. At least, he thought it had been a church at one time. It had a square tower and a graveyard all around it. At the gate stood a pole where a black flag with a white cross fluttered. He was nervous about going inside, but Buzz took his arm and led him in through heavy, metal studded doors, over which was a banner that said 'GREAT OAKS FROM LITTLE ACORNS GROW'.

On the whitewashed walls were brightly coloured murals of

sailing boats and seascapes – Sid thought that's what they were, though to him they were abstract images. He had never been inside an art gallery before. He was hypnotised by the sudden surprise of the paintings.

'Where is everyone?' shouted Buzz.

He led the way between sleeping bags laid out in neat rows to another room behind the main gallery.

'Stash your stuff here if you like.'

Sid removed his blue T-shirt and stuffed it in the backpack. Now Buzz could see the khaki one he had on underneath.

'I like your T, man. Where did you get it? Army, isn't it?'

'A Reducer gave it me,' Sid boasted.

'A Reducer? Really? Wow. *I'm* going to be a Reducer when I grow up.'

Just then a load of boys ran into the main hall, laughing and joshing.

'Hey, Buzz, you're in for it. You should have been in the fields with us.'

'Who's he? Is that a real rifle? Is he TA?'

'Don't be stupid. He's too young.' They jostled close to him.

'This is Sid and he's my friend,' said Buzz.

Sid tried to look fierce and unafraid of this crowd of mud-caked boys, all with shaved heads, like Buzz.

'Can I touch it?' a freckled boy pushed his way forward. They all wanted to touch the rifle.

One bigger boy pushed roughly through the group.

'Out of my way, people.' A path opened up for him. He stood in front of Sid. 'Who said you could come in here without permission?'

'New recruit, Captain. I found him.' Buzz placed a proprietary arm around Sid's shoulder.

Sid had never seen such a handsome boy as the one who stood in front of him. He had deep blue eyes and long dark curling lashes, like a girl's. His lips were full and pink. He was muscular and tall and he looked as if he had never been hungry in his life. He was the only one of the boys who had hair. And what thick curly blonde hair – like a girl's.

The youth grabbed Sid's ID badge that hung around his neck. 'What's this?' He had found Lo's ID, that hung behind Sid's.

'It's my baby sister's. She's been taken away.'

'Like mine,' whispered the freckled boy.

'And mine,' said a sturdy kid with dark tanned skin.

The boys went quiet, some sniffed and brushed their cheeks, and slipped away, some to the showers to wash off the mud of their labours, some straight to their sleeping bags, where they lay with their faces pressed into the floor, their narrow shoulders shaking.

'Have a shower and I'll find you somewhere to kip,' said the big boy gruffly. 'I'm Sergeant Rook.' He put out his arm and shook Sid's hand. 'If you stay you'll have to have a new name.'

'We'll see,' Sid said, echoing his father's words.

'We'll see,' Dad had said.

What was the question? His mother had been attending to his father's injuries. Sid hadn't been watching. No way did he want to know the extent of his dad's disabilities. He only knew his father could no longer walk. A blanket usually covered his father's thin lap. It was Sid's job to keep Lo amused. He read to her to make her sleep. Remembering when his father had read to him at night, at first it had seemed an honour to do this – to read fairy stories to the small girl, to pretend to be a man. But later, he had come to resent the task; he wanted to be out, playing football in the streets, with boys his own age. Why should he have to baby-sit? Some of his friends had left a year before The Emergency. Gone to stay with family in other countries. Or just disappeared. He didn't understand, but recognised the atmosphere of fear that enveloped the city. Shops closed without notice. There was a sudden shortage of basic foods – flour, salt, sugar, cooking oil. No more food deliveries were made to supermarkets. Because there was no more petrol. His mother kept him off school to help in the search for food supplies. Every day they went further afield for rice, flour, sugar, tinned goods and salt.

'What's for sale?' He'd asked a thin man at the end of a seemingly endless line of disconsolate people.

'Dunno, mate, tinned tomatoes, I think.'

So he'd joined the queue and waited two hours to get candles and matches, not tomatoes. That's where he'd heard the rumours: people suspected of being illegals were taken to Holding camps outside the city, where they were assessed, let go or disappeared.

Sid remembered why his father had said, 'We'll see.'

'If we don't go now it'll be too late,' Mam had warned.

'We'll see,' his father had said, 'We'll see.'

Mam had been right. They should have gone away. They might have survived if they had left. Sid went over and over the events of those last few days in the city in his mind. How one day everything went on as normal, and the next there was The Emergency. How the streets were full of the noise of gunshots and tanks and people running and screaming. And even when the TA came to their door, Dad had not believed it was happening. 'Bloody barbarians!' he had called them, turning his wheelchair this way and that. Looking for a way out.

He could still see his mother's face and hear her screams, and her last words to him – 'Take care of my baby, save Lo!'

Rook was a big strong boy, a head taller than Sid. He stood next to him at the soup kitchen.

'In Repops you get privileges.'

'What's Repops?'

'That's what we are. Repops. Chosen to repopulate Earth when it's ready. Have to be healthy, eat properly, do exercise, fight, work hard at lessons, learn the rules, help grow things, do all sorts of stuff. Didn't you belong to a Repop group before you came here?'

'No, I didn't realise...' Sid thought of the feral kids in the city. Runners and Legals were all mixed up together. Here in the Far West the authorities seemed to be more organised. 'Why aren't there any girls?'

'Girls? Who needs them? Their groups are elsewhere in Fort K.'

'What's Fort K?'

'Fortress Kernow, what used to be Cornwall. Don't you even know that?'

'I've been travelling. Are they eight to fourteen?'

'Yeah, same as us. No other kids allowed to stay. We're special.'

'What about all those people in the pool? Who are they?'

'TA. Army. In charge. Have to have someone in charge.'

'What happened to your parents?' Sid asked.

'TA. Colonels, both of them.' Rook looked proud. 'Yours?'

Sid said nothing. His throat had tightened and he couldn't speak as. He brought out the photograph and showed it to Rook. Rook held the photograph and nodded, smiling.

They took their vegetable soup and sat at a bench. Buzz sat on Sid's other side, slurping his soup and dipping his lump of bread in it. Sid gulped his portion and wondered at his good luck. He had fallen on his feet. He had a sleeping bag, food, water, and the company of other boys.

'You'll need to be signed in properly,' said Rook.

'Will I?'

'Yes, of course, so you get a uniform and a card.'

'Got a card.' He held out the laminated ID disk around his neck.

'You need another one.' Buzz slipped a hand into the neck of his T-shirt and pulled out the cord holding his ID. 'A Repop card. Entitles you to free food, vits and soy milk. Repop Rations. They have to keep us fit.'

'Vits?'

'Vitamins, supplements.' He punched Sid on the arm. 'Build you up, kid. You're too small and skinny.' He sniffed suspiciously. 'Better have a shower before we introduce you to the TA.'

At the TA HQ – a crumbling, disused seawater swimming pool, built in the 1930s, Sid was told to stand at attention. The TA officer was a straight-backed woman. Her eyes were the palest grey, almost colourless, her camouflage uniform immaculately clean and pressed. She looked him up and down.

'Name?' She didn't smile.

'Sidney Kingdom Freeman. Sidney after Mam's father. Dad chose Kingdom after Brunel.' He thought of the bridge collapsing. The huge waves born of the falling super-structure. It could be worse. His parents could have called him Isambard.

'I didn't ask for your family history, thank you. Date of birth?'

'09.04.2076. Same birthday as Isambard Kingdom Brunel.

Different year, obviously.'

'Who? Never mind. You're small for your age. ID?'

He showed her his ID. Lo's disk he had put into his backpack before the interview. He wondered why no one had checked his microchip. It would give his entire medical history. Why they had to have all this other stuff was beyond him.

'Address?' Sid told her and she said, 'You're a long way from home, aren't you? Why?'

'Looking for someone.'

A woman sat tapping at a typewriter, pushing the lever over every time she reached the end of a line. She looked up and then went back to her typing.

'Well, if you want to be with Newlyn North Repops you'll have to work hard. No skiving off looking for friends.'

'Okay.' He shrugged.

'You must answer "Yes, Ma'am." And I believe you have a rifle.' It wasn't a question.

'It's mine. I found it.'

'No firearms allowed in Repops.'

'But...'

She raised a white eyebrow towards a guard, who produced Sid's rifle like a rabbit from a magician's hat.

'You may keep the other things, except for the photograph.'

The guard put her hand deep into the pocket of Sid's baggies, and removed the picture of his parents.

'But...'

'You're starting a new life in Repops. Have to forget about the old one, don't we? Clean slate?' She sounded slightly less stern as she said these words. 'Check his chip,' she nodded to the guard, who stepped forward and buzzed Sid's neck with a chip wand and showed the results to her superior.

'I see you've had your malaria, cholera and flu jabs, that's good. AOK.'

Sid's parents had known many people who had died in the great Cow Flu pandemic – Dad's parents, Dad's brother, Uncle Bill, along with a third of the world's population. Little good had it done his parents to survive, he thought, bitterly.

Back at Newlyn North Camp Sid was ordered to strip and one of the women hosed him down. The water smelt of carbolic. He tried to hide his privates from her, and she laughed at him.

'Seen it all before, boy, don't you worry.'

Another woman shaved his head. Her hands, though rough, moved his head gently this way and that. She even smiled at him.

'You'll do, squirt,' she said and rubbed his head. He sniffed and grinned at her.

The guard locked the rifle away in a cupboard and presented him with cap, shorts, shirt and a tag with a number on it and marched him back to the gallery. It wasn't until he was back in his sleeping bag and he went automatically to look at the photo in his baggies before he went to sleep that he realised the enormity of his loss. How had they known about the picture? There was only one other boy who knew about it. Rook! Rook must have informed on him. He'd pretended to be friendly when all the time he was spying on him.

At lights out Rook locked the door and kept the key on a string around his neck. Sid lay awake, boiling with anger. He had walked into a trap. Perhaps he wouldn't be able to find his grandparents, or go back for Lo.

At 0700 hours, after raising the Repops flag and saluting it, they mustered for morning exercises, which lasted three hours. After marching like soldiers through the town, they jogged for three miles cross-country (nowhere near Freedom Farm, Sid noticed), chanting songs to keep in step. Back at the camp breakfast was porridge, brown toast and a thin scraping of peanut paste washed down with apple flavoured vitamin drink.

Most mornings Sid went with a small group to do work experience in the fields. In the afternoon he sat in an airless classroom. He preferred digging, planting and hoeing, to being talked at about citizenship and politics. Hard physical labour and a full stomach suited him. However, guilt and remorse would return at night, as he lay in his sleeping bag, worrying about Lo. He shouldn't have left her. Anything could have happened. How would he know if the TA had found them, if the Reducers had raided? His mother would never forgive him if Lo came to harm.

But like the other boys he giggled about Ms Pigeon's large breasts and bum, and had occasional romantic thoughts about the younger of the female teachers – Ms Gull, with her golden hair and snub nose. And he still thought about the daisy girl. Nights were worst because of the other boys crying. Some cried out in their sleep for their mothers. Sid still felt bitter about his photo. They shouldn't have done that, he thought. Taking away my past, my family. I'll never forget Mam and Dad, no matter what.

He imagined Lo in green shorts being a Forest Fairy and playing with other little girls and hoped she was happy and hadn't forgotten him. She'd have a new name now. He hoped she knew the daisy girl and had told her about her older brother, how he was her hero!

He had a new name, Starling, which he thought was ridiculous, but Buzz soon shortened it to Starl and then Star, and all the others apart from Rook, called him Star, which made him feel better.

'Could have been worse. They could have called you Blue-tit, or Great-tit!' Buzz wrestled Sid to the ground.

He didn't trust Rook after his photo was confiscated, and tried to have nothing to do with him.

But the Reducer's khaki T-shirt gave him kudos of a sort, like a war medal. They hadn't taken that away. Or the sunglasses.

One night, the boys all in their sleeping bags, Buzz asked him to tell the story of how he had saved the Reducer's life. Rook, in the only camp bed, by the door, pretended not to listen, but the other boys were impressed. Sid omitted Lo from the narrative, letting them believe that she had been taken with his parents in the original Reduction. She would be safer if no one knew that she was close by. He couldn't trust anyone not to give her away. Would he ever be able to find Freedom Farm again? He felt sure he would. In his head was a vague map of West Penwith, the big town of Penzance, with Marazion a few miles along the same softer, wooded coast, and then the boulder-strewn moors rising to windy heights with views of valleys plunging to the other bleaker terrain of the peninsular to the north. At its narrowest he reckoned it was about eight miles across as the crow flies.

'Hey, look what I found,' Buzz whispered, shoving the tattered remains of a comic book under Sid's nose. 'Spiderman!'

'Yeah, where did you get it?'

'Found it.'

Sid thought about the Spiderman suit he'd had when he was four. Ten years ago. He wouldn't take it off. He'd even worn it to bed. A bit like Lo and her fairyprincessdress. And he thought about something his father had said when he was thirteen, when his mam was worried about his obsession with Brunel.

'We all need heroes,' his dad had said.

'Listen up, people, stop yammering. Lights out.' Rook barked from his bed. Buzz crept back to his sleeping bag and hid the fragile comic in the torn lining.

With exercise and good food Sid put on muscle. He was no longer the puny lad he had been when he arrived twelve weeks before. Lo wouldn't recognise him, he thought. At least he didn't have head lice any more. There was nowhere for them to hide on his shaved head. He still hadn't any new body hair, while Rook had the enviable signs of pale fluff on his upper lip and his voice was sometimes as deep as a man's.

One day, marching with his team along the old promenade, past the sea defences of piled-up broken vehicles, coastguard vessels patrolling the bumpy sea beyond the harbour, they saw a women being chased by soldiers. She was younger than the women who were in charge of the Repops, and obviously pregnant.

A Runner.

Sid didn't see what happened because they went into another road, but he heard the shots. All the boys were subdued that evening in the gallery.

He still didn't allow himself to think about his parents and what might have happened to them.

One evening, exhausted after toiling in the hot dusty fields all day, he and Buzz were sitting in the same little park where they had first met. He hadn't seen much of Buzz these past weeks, as the younger boy had been in a different work group until now. Swarms of gnats hovered around their sweaty heads. The boys were trying to make a sound from stems of grass held between their fingers and put to their lips. As they blew obscene sounds came from their mouths and they giggled.

'You from round here then, Buzz?'

'Nah, man, I'm from Mousehole.' (He pronounced it Muzzel). 'Where's that?'

'Next village. Little harbour, boats an' that. Ma and Dad in tourism.'

'What, a guest house?'

'Green tourism. Yurt village like.'

Sid thought of the tents and yurt he had seen at Freedom Farm.

'Were they reduced?'

'Nah, Runners. But not me. I wanted to stay. Anyway, I'm legal, aren't I?'

'Where are they now, do you know?'

'Dunno, do I?'

'Don't you miss them?'

'Yeah, I suppose.' Buzz looked down thoughtfully, then said, 'Good life here though?'

'Yeah, I suppose it is. When we going to meet girls then?'

'Who cares, man? Got Ms Gull, innit?' Buzz made an obscene gesture.

'Yeah, who cares?'

Muzzel, Sid thought. Another town with a 'z' in it. Two even.

One week they spent each day on the slate roofs of the town, painting them white. Most of the Repops enjoyed this, even though it was hard, hot work. In the cool of the early mornings and late evenings they leapt from roof to roof, swung from old chimney pots, slid down sloping roofs before grabbing onto rickety guttering and swinging themselves up to safety. Roof-running was dangerous and exhilarating. Sid was one of the best. Being small and neatly made, he was supple and athletic.

One evening, as the sun was disappearing over the distant hills and the air was cooling, they were playing tag on the way back to the headquarters, as usual. But it was rather slippery after a sharp rain shower and one of the older boys, a clumsy lad called Stonechat (who they called Chatty, because he was) slid down a roof and fell to the ground.

'Don't move him,' ordered Rook and sent one of the smaller boys to fetch the TA. But it was a long time before they came and lifted him onto a stretcher and took him away. Chatty was still alive, moaning horribly.

All the boys were all shocked by the incident.

'What's the point of painting roofs, anyway?' said Buzz, rubbing his aching arm. He had white paint spattered all over his face and arms.

'The Warming. White paint reflects heat back into the sky. We did it ages ago where I lived.'

Sid wondered why there still wasn't enough power. Occasionally they had power at night, but more often than not the lights wouldn't come on at all. At least here by the sea there were fewer mosquitoes and flies than in the city and no shortage of food.

'Is Chat going to be OK?' Sid asked Rook a couple of days after the accident.

Rook looked at him strangely. 'Don't be so naive, Starling. He'll have been reduced. What good is he with a broken back?'

Sid went cold with horror. Of course, that's what they would have done with Dad, too. He was useless to Fortress Kernow without his legs. He admitted the worst to himself and felt terribly alone.

On fieldwork weeks they marched two by two, hoes, spades and forks over their shoulders, back to the fields each day. They sang. They didn't know where the song came from. School? Childhood? *Hey ho, hey ho, it's off to work we go.* He thought of little Lo singing it with him; he thought of the roundabout and Mal the Reducer.

An incident occurred one damp humid day: Sparra stuck himself through the foot with a garden fork. Right through. He fainted over the fork, his foot still stuck to the earth. No hesitation, Sid (he still thought of himself as Sid) drew out the tines smoothly, held the boy as he fell, and called for help.

Rook came up to him later in the high fields.

'The lad's going to be fine. You did well, Starling,' he said. 'I think you're probably officer material.'

'Me?'

'Yes. I have observed that you're admired by the men,' (Little kids, Sid thought) 'and you have leadership qualities.'

'Would I be able to grow my hair like you?'

'Yes, it's one of the privileges that officers have.'

Sid's heart swelled. He was beginning to enjoy being with these boys – men. He was going to be a leader of men. If he played his cards right. If he learned enough. If he kept on the right side of Rook. If he worked hard, did as he was told. Maybe one day he could train to be a Reducer? Wear black leathers, ride a powerful motorbike, fire guns. Get tattooed. Grow a beard. He felt more cheerful than he had felt since the day when the bridges had come down.

I'm stronger than Dad, he thought. He pushed the unspoken betrayal away. Of course he was physically stronger than Dad; who wouldn't be? He remembered his father reading to him when he was little. Before he had had his accident he had played football with his son, taught him about all sorts of things – politeness to his elders and betters, how to cut bread, how to hold a cricket bat, how to tie a knot, how to build a bridge of bricks, how to admit when he was wrong, and respect for his mother. Sid couldn't actually remember what else, but he knew that his father had shown him how to be a man.

Sid tried to remember his mother's smile, the smile in the photograph, thin and hopeful, her dark wavy hair under the thrown-back wedding veil, but he couldn't. Only her bitten lips and the frown lines she had worn between her eyebrows since Dad's accident. In a way, the accident had eclipsed The Emergency, when they were herded with neighbours and strangers into the newly formed ghetto. The accident happened at the same time, so that when he was discharged from hospital, instead of going home to Brunel Avenue, it was to the ghetto.

Life had changed overnight for Sid. No more yard to play in, or room of his own. He had to share with his little sister. And he often missed school to go with his mother to search for basic food.

It made him sad to think about his parents, but he knew he should remember as much as he could so that he could tell Lo when she asked. If she asked.

It hit him that he was the man of the family now. And he remembered his mother's plea to him to look after Lo. The responsibility was like a heavy weight hanging around his neck. Shame made him blush as if his thoughts had been spoken aloud. How could he even for a moment have wanted to be a Reducer?

The first opportunity he had to look for his grandparents' house, he took off at a trot. Once a week each boy had two hours' leave from Repop duties. He headed for the further part of town, where there were rows of houses on a hill, because he remembered a hill. He was searching for a large monkey puzzle tree in a small front garden, but most of the front gardens were given over to veggie plots. Empty houses had been burnt to the ground or left derelict, with wheel-less rusting vehicles collapsed on cement drives. There were no monkey puzzle trees to be seen. The tree he was looking for had been a strange shape, like a pine tree but with very spiky branches. No way could you climb it; there weren't even birds' nests in it. it was pretty useless really. But his grandmother had been proud of it. She was short-tempered, couldn't be doing with kids. Grumps, Dad called her. Gramps was all right though.

He walked disconsolately up and down for a mile or so, until he got to the town centre again, and the swimming pool. He was sure he would find it eventually, but time was running out. He had to report back at 0900. It was best to search in the early part of the day, before it became too hot. With thirty minutes left, he ran beyond the pool towards the other side of town.

'What are you doing, boy? Aren't you supposed to be in camp?' A short belligerent man in TA fatigues stopped him by jabbing him in the chest with a leather riding crop.

'Sir,' Sid stood to attention and saluted. 'On morning leave, Sir.'

'Show me your ID, boy.'

He eventually let him go, but Sid had lost precious time. He would have to try again another day.

One day, Sid was working on his own at the edge of a field, mending a dry-stone hedge, placing chunks of granite into the gaps, and thinking about Isambard Kingdom Brunel. How he would have enjoyed mending this wall, because that was what he was good at, building things. Sid did what he often did before The Emergency, he pretended Brunel was there chatting to him.

'*Hello lad, it's Sid, isn't it? Knew your father. Good man. Sorry about his accident.*'

'Yeah, thanks, sir. He admired you above all other men.'

'*Did he?*'

'Mr Brunel – I wonder if you might be able to help me? You being a famous engineer.'

'*Call me Izzi,*' Brunel wore a tall black hat with a narrow rim, a waistcoat under a long jacket and smoked a cigar.

'Oh I couldn't do that, sir. You're a famous dead person.'

'*Do call me Izzi, my boy. Makes me feel more alive, if you know what I mean.*'

'Who are you talking to, man?' It was Buzz.

'No one, myself. Bad habit.' Sid scratched his shaved head, embarrassed.

'I talk to my little sister, sometimes.' Buzz did a one-hand handstand and leapt up again.

'Didn't know you had a sister. What's her name?'

'Dolphin.'

'Dolphin? Isn't that a fish?'

'I dunno. It's her name but I called her Doll. Anyway, we've all been given the names of birds.'

'Yeah, suppose.'

'What sort of a fish is a dolphin, then?' asked Buzz.

'Big, fast, jumps out of water, smiles. Or did. It's extinct,' he told the younger boy.

'Smiles? Doll smiles a lot.'

'Good name for her then, innit? What do you talk about?'

'Stuff. Things what happen. Tell her what I'm doing, where I am.'

'How old is she?'

'Three. She can talk and stuff. They took her with them when they ran.' He sniffed and blinked fast.

'Girls are different from us,' said Sid. He thought about Lo, her love of pink things, being a little mother to her dolls, wanting to play tea parties. She didn't like guns and football or building things. But his mother didn't fit. She hadn't been a girly sort of mother. She had played rugby with a women's team. Did weightlifting. Was good at putting up shelves and mending things. He tried to remember the last time she had kissed him goodnight. She used to read to him when he was little, before Dad's accident, before Lo was born. Then she would kiss him. *Good night, sleep tight, don't let the bugs bite.* He choked back a tear and sniffed hard and noticed that Buzz was having trouble in that department too.

CHAPTER SEVENTEEN

JUST LATELY ROOK was making a point of sitting with Sid at mealtimes. In spite of himself, Sid was flattered. But he was wary, also. He wouldn't give anything away about Lo.

'Tell us how you came to be with the Reducer then, Starling.'

'Didn't I say?'

'Missed it.'

'He came off his Harley. I looked after him.'

'Where were you?'

'East of here.'

'Yeah? Where exactly?'

'I don't know. Woods.'

'So where is he now?'

'Dunno. Went back to his squad. Why do you want to know?'

'Why were you there? Were you hiding, or what?'

'On my way west.'

'Why?'

'Told you. My grandparents are here somewhere.'

'But why weren't you put with Repops where you lived?'

'Dunno, a mix-up. Anyway, had adventures.' Sid sniffed.

'So, what was the Reducer's name?'

'Mal.'

'Mal? That means bad.'

'Does it? Well, he wasn't bad. Taught me to shoot and how to build an earth oven.' Sid thought of Mal with sudden affection, as if he were an uncle or an old family friend.

'Malodorous – bad smelling; malnutrition – faulty nutrition; malfunction – not working. Maladjusted. Like you, see?' Rook dug Sid in the ribs.

Sid grunted. Rook was too clever. He didn't trust him. Never would he forgive him for telling about the photograph. It was malicious, malevolent, maltreatment.

In the musty classroom there was the high whine of mosquitoes, and the smell of feet. Sid fought off sleep. The lecture was on the onset of Climate Change.

'So, as I explained before, when the ice-caps completely melted during the second half of the twenty-first century sea levels rose by seven metres worldwide. 2055 – the turning point for civilisation. Write down that date in your books.' Ms Thrush waved away a fly buzzing close to her face and turned her gaze on the boys.

Sid already knew that. He had been taught all about Climate Change at his school in the city.

'Entire nations moved to higher ground. The world suddenly shrunk to far fewer suitable habitats for animals and humans.'

A murmur went round the room.

'I think Ms Gull has told you all about the CCP? The Chemical Castration Programme?' They nodded, squirming in embarrassment.

'Any questions?' Ms Thrush asked.

Sid raised his hand. 'Please Miss, why didn't they sterilise women instead of reducing them?'

'Good question, Starling. It happened at first, of course, when the Population Reduction Programme began, but it became obvious that there would still be far too many people to feed.'

The boys fidgeted in the heat. Blue-bottles zig-zagged across the room, banging against the dusty windows.

'Even when the great Cow Flu pandemic killed millions worldwide,' she continued, rapping her stick on the front desk, causing the sleepy boy who sat there to jump, 'many nations banned couples from having more than one child. Some low IQ couples were not allowed to have any. But still there was not enough water and food for everyone. So, the obvious had to happen. Breeding was forbidden.'

Sparra started to chortle behind his hands.

'Grow up, Sparrow,' she said crossly. 'That still wasn't enough. To simplify, the rulers of all the countries in the world got together and came to the conclusion that only solution for the survival of Earth, and incidentally for the survival of mankind, was to rapidly reduce numbers to save a few: a special few, of whom you are among the… er… chosen,' she stuttered to a halt. 'Silence!' She pointed to a boy at the back.

'How come you weren't reduced, Miss?'

'Any *intelligent* questions?'

'I can see why I was chosen,' said a hefty boy called Jay, 'but why choose that lot?' He swept his arm round to include the entire class, who jeered and clapped and laughed at his insult.

'Healthy, fit and bright boys and girls between the ages of eight and fourteen are going to be the parents of the future.' Sweat glistened on her high forehead. She was losing control of the class, and knew it. 'It will be up to your generation, when the time comes, to be ready to do the right thing for humanity.'

'Sleep with a lot of girls,' quipped Finch.

'Okay, that's enough, boys, that's enough.' The teacher rapped her cane on the desk. They eventually calmed down.

'How many people are left in Fort K, Miss?' Sid didn't know the boy who'd raised his hand.

'Enough to grow food, Robin, do other vital work, guard our water supplies, guard our borders, be involved with food and biogas security, work at recycling metals and other vital products, and the important job of teaching and caring for the chosen Repops.'

And kill Runners, thought Sid.

'Why do people want to get into Fort K, Miss? Aren't they being looked after in their own zones?' the same boy asked.

'All the eastern counties of England, Ireland, Wales and Scotland were badly affected by the initial flooding. Whole cities and towns disappeared, including London, which used to be the capital city, as I'm sure you know. We grow plenty of food in Fortress Kernow, enough to feed the local population, but no more. And more importantly, we have…? What do we have?' She pointed at a gingery boy in the back row who was almost asleep. His neighbour jabbed at him.

'Dunno, Miss. Seagulls?'

The boys fell about laughing.

'Water, Crow, we have fresh water. Without fresh water everything dies. Cornwall, I mean Fortress Kernow, has always had a high rainfall, and luckily that hasn't changed much over the years, in spite of The Warming.'

'But shouldn't we look after starving people, Miss? And people with no water?'

'Unfortunately, Sparrow, in order to survive we can no longer allow more people in.'

The class murmured and fidgeted in the hot and airless room. Ms Thrush fanned herself with her notes and frowned.

'If I leave Fort Kernow, can I come back again?' asked Finch, slapping at a mosquito on his leg.

'Not until The Emergency is over. Travel is forbidden.'

A boy at the back raised his hand. 'Does that mean the starving will die, Miss?'

'There was plenty of warning of what was in store for the world's populations, Swan. Scientists had told governments, but people didn't want to believe in the coming hardships for the human race.

'Droughts caused grain crops to fail. Civil wars broke out when food stocks fell and prices rose. Many bad things happened, but in spite of low-lying countries disappearing under the waves, many countries are still capable of supporting life: large parts of Russia, Siberia, Canada, Tibet, China, the Yukon, Newfoundland, New Zealand, Finland, Norway and Sweden.' She sighed, turned away and rubbed off the map from the blackboard. 'Wales, Ireland and Scotland. the Arctic, the Antarctic,' she hesitated, searching for more names. 'Lots of places.' She coughed and raised her hand. 'Class dismissed.' She shuffled her papers and shoved them into a briefcase, then wiped the perspiration from her brow.

The boys all started talking at once. How were survivors going to get to habitable zones, thought Sid, if no one's allowed to fly or sail or drive any more? Walk? Well, he and Lo had.

After lessons the boys ran around the graveyard, kicking footballs, wrestling, the younger ones swapping glass marbles. One boy was trying to catch a butterfly in a net on a pole. He chased the small blue butterfly across graves. Sid tried to help by waving his arms at the insect as it flew close to him. He tripped on a flat gravestone and fell heavily, scraping his hands and elbows. When he sat up he saw the inscription:

JOSEPH SIDNEY JENKYN

BORN JUNE 2024

FELL ASLEEP SEP 2089

RIP

What RIP meant he had no idea. He stared at the black stone with the jar of dead flowers at its head. He had died last year. The evidence had been under Sid's nose all this time and he hadn't seen it.

He sat down by the grave. This was a disaster. It meant that he had nowhere to take Lo. He couldn't imagine his grumpy grandmother wanting to hide and look after a five-year-old. He sat for a while thinking about Gramps. His hairy ears and nostrils. He liked a snooze in the afternoon. He snored, coughed a lot, sucked peardrops. Sid could hardly remember him really. He squeezed out a few tears, but they were for himself. He tried to remember what his mam had said about her parents. They'd worked in a mycoculture production factory for years – glorified mushroom farm, Dad had called it – and then ran a recycling unit. Perhaps if he could find an antique telephone directory, he could look up recycling units in Fort Kernow. Maybe that was the way to find them – her. If he wanted to. And maybe Grumps would come to visit the grave? People did that. He could watch out for her. If he really wanted to find her... but did he?

'Come on Star, race you to the harbour.'

Sid rose and ran after Buzz to the harbour wall, where they sat and counted the coastguard vessels patrolling the coast, rowed by teams of muscled men and women, and breathed in the salt air.

At least here there was a cool breeze.

'What do you want to be when you grow up, Star?' Buzz asked.

'Dunno.' Most of his boyhood he had wanted to be the next Isambard Kingdom Brunel. But now maybe he could be a coastguard or a border guard, a policeman or a fire-fighter? Yeah, a fire-fighter would be exciting. He would have to join the TA first of course; they would teach him how to be a fireman.

'Fire-fighter,' he announced.

'Reducer, me.'

'You told me, yeah. You want to kill people do you?'

The boy giggled in embarrassment. 'They get to drive fast motorbikes; they got guns, man.'

'Yeah, and they get to kill mothers and fathers and little kids.'

'No they don't. They get to round them up so they can be taken to Sunshine Camps.'

'Who told you that?'

'Dunno.'

'There are no Sunshine Camps, Buzz. There's only us and them – Repops and the TA. Reducers are part of the TA.'

'Don't believe you. I'll ask Fat Ass.'

'What do you think Reducer means?'

'A bloke what finds people and sends them to Sunshine Camps where they get to eat less so that they become thinner.'

'Have you ever seen a Sunshine Camp?'

Buzz shook his head.

Sid sighed. 'To reduce is to make smaller. Population Reduction is about cutting down the numbers of the population – the people who live here. That's what Runners are running from.'

'But, isn't that murder?'

'Yeah, it's murder.'

'But they get paid to do it?'

'Yeah, they get paid to do it.' He thought about Mal, the glossy Harley motorbike, the leathers, the tattoos. Part of Sid admired the Reducer.

'I know a secret,' said the younger boy.

'What secret?'

'Let me have your T-shirt and I'll tell you.'

'Joking aren't you?'

'Yeah, man, joking.' Buzz punched him lightly on the arm and they began to play fight. When they had had enough rough and tumble, Sid removed the khaki T. ' Here, you can have a go of it for today if you like.'

'Really? Thanks, Star.' He tore off his own shirt and pulled the Reducer's T-shirt over his head. It came down to his knees, hiding his shorts completely. They both laughed.

Running back to Newlyn North Repop Camp Buzz told his secret.

'I heard Fat Ass talking to Ms Gull about an island. Scilly, it's called, off Land's End. She said there are loads of Runners there, and no one bothers about them.'

'How do they live?'

'Like smugglers, wreckers, like in the old days.'

'No ships to wreck,' sneered Sid. 'Anyway, I thought all islands were flooded.'

'Most are. Not that one though.'

'How did they get there?'

'Lived there before The Emergency? Stole a boat and sailed there?'

That night before he slept, Sid surrounded himself in a new fantasy. His parents had escaped the Reducers and found their way to the safe island, where they waited for him and Lo. They grew all their own food and had a farm like Old MacDonald. Dad had miraculously recovered the use of his legs or grown some new ones. His mam was happy and pretty again, like she used to be. They all lived in a stone cottage overlooking the sea. He had a red dog and Lo had a white kitten. They stayed on the beach all day. He woke and for a brief moment thought it was true. Then he cried silently.

Weeks passed without Sid having decided what to do about Lo, or looking for his grandmother. Maybe he would stay here forever, be looked after and fed. He had friends, he was learning new skills – how to sow seed and prick out seedlings, how to ride a horse and drive it between the shafts of a plough, how to gather crops and sort them, how to store them so they wouldn't rot.

Some days he made a point of visiting the grave of Joseph Sidney Jenkyn, in case his grandmother had come to pay her respects. He even went as far as (when no one was watching) to place some cowslips on the grave. But he never saw her, and, in fact, was quite relieved.

One day there was a football match between his camp and Penzance East. It was played on an old car park by the harbour, the tarmac split by grass and rose-bay willow-herb. The other boys cheered and shouted encouragement. Rook, the captain, was a speedy and accurate right-winger, and with his help Sid scored two goals. Five minutes before the final whistle the scores were even. Sid took a cunning cross from Rook, performed a brilliant dribble past the big, red-faced defender, did a clever back-flip and scored, winning the game for Newlyn North.

The captain of Penzance East, a heavy-set boy with big hands and feet and bad acne, came up to Sid and whispered in his ear – 'I'll get you for that, Smiler.'

'Well played, people. Well done, Star,' said Rook, slapping him on the back. Sid's heart swelled with pride. Rook had called him Star, not Starling. Lifted onto two boys' shoulders Sid was carried off, man of the match.

The best lessons were in fighting skills. Recently each boy had been issued with his own wooden lance, longer and as nearly as thick as the handle of a broom, sharpened at both ends, and each boy had customised his lance, some with string or ribbon, some with colour. Sid had carved his name in full along the length of his – Sidney Kingdom Freeman – followed by a five-pointed star. He kept it by his side always. He was also taught how to fight with his feet and hands.

One rest period, instead of lying around doing nothing, roof-running, or playing football, Sid went off on his own looking for the house with the monkey puzzle tree. Just in case he ever needed to know where it was. His search took him to a part of town he hadn't been to before in the east of the town. He was climbing a hill, balancing one point of his fighting lance on the palm of one hand, about to give up the search, and thinking that it was time to get back to camp, when a gang of boys, all carrying sharpened lances, appeared from a side alley. They surrounded him.

'Well, well, well! It's Smiler!' The big boy with acne announced with satisfaction. Sid's heart beat fast. He could have run away. He stood his ground.

'So what?' he said.

'So, where's the rest of your team now?'

'You're a bad loser, Bigfoot.'

The object of Sid's remark stood with his large feet wide apart and twirled his lance aggressively. The gang drew back to give him room. Sid prepared himself for action.

Although his opponent was physically more powerful, Sid was lighter on his feet. He ducked and weaved, springing backwards and sideways as the bully advanced, meeting lance with lance.

'Got you now,' Bigfoot gloated.

Cornered in the alley, Sid leapt onto a garden wall and cracked his adversary on the head. In retaliation he jabbed the spike at Sid's legs.

'Kill him, kill him,' the boys yelled at their leader. But Sid had the edge on him, and was above him. He took aim and threw the lance. It found its target: the upper arm took the blow. Bigfoot dropped his own weapon and fell, grunting in agony. Sid jumped down, pushed down on the injured boy's shoulder with one foot, drew out the lance and quickly climbed onto the wall again. Blood oozed out of Bigfoot's arm. The point had hit muscle. He writhed around on the pavement, his pals around him. One of them lunged at Sid, taking him by surprise and Sid's lance clattered out of his hands. He sprang down from the wall and performed several quick karate chops, felling his attacker and two other boys who had tried to restrain him. Retrieving his weapon he slipped away, dashing along walls and balancing along fences, running through alleys and back lanes, leaping over invisible mines and dodging an imaginary foe. Striding, chest out, head held high, he became in quick succession a Samurai warrior, a pirate, a musketeer, a spaceman, Spiderman, a saviour of mothers and fathers and small children who would have been reduced but for his courage; loved forever by the girl with daisies in her hair; loved by all Runners, everywhere; until he was back safe in Newlyn North Repop territory, bruised but jubilant, triumphant.

Next day Sid was put in charge of a team of five younger boys and given the task of clearing rocks and boulders from a field so it could be ploughed and used for growing food crops. They worked well in the early morning before it became too hot, shifting the smaller stones to the edges. There was one large boulder that they were having trouble with. It was covered in lichens: green hairy ones, yellow ones like gold flakes, and white ones like splashes of paint. They had managed to lever it up on one side but it was still stuck fast in the earth. Buzz, being one of the more skinny boys, offered to get under it and dig it out while the others held it up. He was digging away with a small spade, trying to loosen the base of the boulder, which had sat there for a thousand years and didn't want to be moved. Two earthworms wriggled out of the sudden blinding light where they had been thrust, back into the dark soil. No birds sang in the humid heat. No breeze blew, even on the high moor. Only gnats and midges hovered around the boys' heads. Bluebottles drank the sweat on their arms and legs.

'Can't hold it much longer,' said Sparra, and promptly slid over, letting go his leverage pole. The others couldn't hang on without him and the boulder fell on top of Buzz, who screamed, and didn't stop. With strength he didn't know he had, Sid hefted the boulder up on his own, then ordered the scared boys to hold it up while he dragged the injured boy out.

One leg stuck out at an odd angle and the foot seemed to have turned the wrong way round. They were a mile or so from their camp and there were no adults around. Sid remembered how long the boy with the broken back had had to wait.

'Go tell them that I'm bringing in an injured man, go, run!' The little boys ran, leaving Sid to lift Buzz. He practically ran with him down across the fields to the town, Buzz screaming most of the way, until he passed out with the pain.

Later, the TA officer called all the boys to attention in the camp. She called Sid's name, or rather, she called out 'Repop Cadet Starling!' He stood there for a moment, forgetting that he was now Starling, until pushed forward by the boy behind him.

'Cadet Starling, having considered your exemplary service and attitude, I am promoting you to Corporal.' She leaned over him and pinned a red stripe to his sand coloured shirt. He saluted, smiling broadly and stepped back to loud cheers.

Valerian grew in thick clumps from the dry-stone hedge. Sid watched a pair of adders writhe in a knot in a patch of sun. It was a rare day off and earlier he had visited Buzz in the hospital and taken him a cast-off slow-worm skin he had found in the graveyard. Buzz's broken leg was in plaster and held up at an angle from the bed by a hoist. Hot and uncomfortable, pale and tearful, he was allergic to the antibiotic he had been given to stop infection. He moaned quietly and didn't even seem to recognise his friend. The nurse had told Sid that he mustn't come again. Sparrow was too ill to receive visitors.

'He'll get better, though, won't he? It's only a broken leg.'

The nurse shrugged.

Sid left the fascinating mating of the snakes and wandered off over the hill, thinking about Buzz, what a good little mate he'd always been.

'Kill, kill, kill,' he heard a chorus of small boys yelling. There was the sound of yelping and whining. He ran to where a group of eight-year-old Repops stood in a circle, brandishing sticks, whooping madly. A skinny young dog cowered on the ground as they beat it. It had been dark brown but was now red with blood.

'What are you doing?' he shouted and they stopped briefly to look up, their eyes wide. He tore the stick from one, then another boy, who angrily tried to get it back. Sid lashed out at him in fury.

'Rook said we could reduce it. It's illegal. Not allowed.'

'Bloody barbarians,' Sid conjured up one of his father's expressions. He took off his shirt and wrapped the injured puppy in it.

'We'll tell on you,' a boy shouted after him. He carried the dog back to the church where his backpack was, and bathed its wounds in disinfectant from the first-aid kit. It whined pitifully.

'What are you doing, Sergeant?' It was Rook. 'That dog's illegal. It must be culled.'

Sid ignored him.

'Repops are chosen survivors. We follow orders or we're out. That means you too, Corporal Starling. I shall have to report you to the Commander.'

'Yeah, you do that.' Sid carried on bathing the dog's cuts. It trembled, looking up at him with trusting eyes.

'You'll be stripped of your stripe, Starling. Head shaved.'

'Oh, piss off, Rook. What's the point of being alive if you're inhuman?' He gathered his few belongings, regretting again the loss of the one and only photograph of his parents, and made a sling out of his bloody Repop shirt in which to carry the puppy.

'You lost your mam too, eh?' he whispered to it.

Rook had stomped off to report Starling to his superiors. Sid made for the kitchen, his lance resting on one shoulder, and took some apples and a packet of Kworn, soy biscuits, and a bottle of water. Looking in a drawer he found a metal meat skewer.

He opened the padlock with the point of the skewer. As he thought, his rifle was there still, in the cupboard, with various other confiscated treasures: penknives, catapults, a flick-knife, Buzz's Spiderman comic, and a red model car. He picked up the car and stroked it, admiring the rubber wheels and the opening doors, and put it back regretfully. He took his rifle, the box of lead shot and the flick-knife, feeling very wicked: his mother hated flick-knives, and his father disapproved of boys who carried them. No sign of the photo, though. Before leaving he looked up at a side wall to the only piece of church decoration that had survived the various changes the building had undergone – a carved wooden angel grieving over a list of local war dead.

As soon as he had left the churchyard a fierce looking woman in her early sixties entered with a bunch of wild flowers clutched in her huge red hands. She sucked at her few remaining teeth as she laid the wilting primroses on a grave and squeezed out a few tears. She wondered at the cowslips dying in a dried out jar. Had she put them there? She couldn't remember.

'Joe boy,' she whispered, 'Miss you lots, you old bugger. No news of Janey or the littl'uns. Should have come two years ago when you asked her, shouldn't she? Anyway, I'm praying for them.' She sniffed and scratched her arm where a scabies rash had spread. 'Anyway, got to get back to work.' She put a grubby finger to her lips and blew a kiss. Boys ran about the gravestones, ignoring the woman. After she left, two boys wrestled on the grave scattering the flowers.

Sparrows nested in the space between the roof and the guttering of the hospital and starlings strutted on the paved area in front. Sid felt a sudden affinity with the birds he was named after. He liked their speckled breasts, which, caught by the sun, looked as if they had been knitted from green and gold sparkly wool. They chattered at the sky in whistles and clicks and chirps. Ivy grew all over the walls, hiding the nests of robin and blackbird. There were vegetable plots on three sides. A woman stretched up to gather runner beans from a tepee of bamboo sticks, and he saw blue veins standing out from behind her knees, dark sweat patches under the arms of her faded shirt.

He went into the main entrance and through to the wards, crouching down so the nurse behind the desk wouldn't see him, and sneaked past to the side room where his friend lay under the drapes of a limp mosquito net. The puppy wriggled, its long legs dangling from the makeshift sling. Flies hit at the dusty window. Buzz was on a saline drip, and unconscious. His head had a fuzzy covering of reddish hair. He looked like a young bride under a muslin veil. Like Sid's mam in the photo.

Sid removed the khaki T-shirt from his pack and placed it at the end of the bed with his lance on top of it. 'Just came to say goodbye and good luck,' he murmured, saluted and crept out again.

CHAPTER EIGHTEEN

ON THE HIGH MOOR, a south-westerly breeze cooling his skin, Sid breathed in the scent of gorse flowers. The puppy whined and stuck his dark face out of the sling and tasted the air. He seemed to have recovered from his beating. As gently as he could, Sid emptied him out onto the grass, where the puppy shook himself and woofed. Then he rolled over and offered his pink belly to Sid's hand.

'What's your name then, fella, eh? What'll I call you?' The tall puppy, which was a bit of this and a bit of that, but mostly water spaniel, with dense curly brown hair, licked his wounds briefly and bounded off a little way, and turning, came back to Sid's side and licked the boy's ankle. Sid found a flattish boulder with a shallow hollow in the surface and poured water into it for the dog to lap. It was soon gone and he refilled the natural bowl. When the dog had had his fill, Sid dipped the bloody shirt in the water, swooshed it around, wrung it out and put it on.

They chased butterflies and lounged in the grass, Sid stroking the dog and talking to him, telling him about Lo and how they were going to visit her. He cleared nettles and made a hollow in the shade of a stone hedge, dozed a little, and woke to find the puppy curled up beside him, licking his wounds.

He threw a stick and the puppy ran after it and brought it back to him.

'Is he a good dog then, is he? Is he?' The dog growled happily as Sid fondled him.

'That's what I'll call you – Izzi – after Isambard. We've both got names to live up to, eh?' He scratched the dog on its head and gently squeezed its floppy ears. Izzi licked his face enthusiastically. He's like Lo, Sid thought, he's forgotten his mam already.

After eating an apple and sharing a couple of biscuits with Izzi, he set off again, keeping the sea behind him on one side of the land and the sea in front on the other. Sid whistled softly to himself, content, as he had not been for a long time. Bats jinked in the darkening sky like swallows of the night. He came to a high point and looked down towards a furrowed field where scarecrows were strung up in a row on a fence. Terrified, for a moment he thought they were crucified men. He must be lost. He couldn't recognise any of the landscape. There was no bosky valley planted with nut trees where he expected it to be. Only a windswept moor with stunted thorn trees tortured by the prevailing wind into horizontal forms, like crippled old people. Where was Freedom Farm? He had been sure he had come in the right direction. He was suddenly weary and the little dog was limping, head down, tongue lolling. He picked him up and carried him for a few hundred metres, but still couldn't recognise the rough moorland. He stumbled over rocks and scratched himself as he fought his way through brambles, gorse and bracken, the still blood-soaked shirt torn and sweat-stained.

They spent the night under a hedge, close to the hidden nest of a skylark that kept very still and quiet, its small heart beating fast under pale feathers. While they slept a meteor shower lit the sky briefly like a far-off firework display. A barn owl silently lifted a vole from the cracked earth. Rabbits munched on the grass by the faint blue light of stars.

That same day Lo had been learning to read and write with Sweetpea and Sand in the shade of the spreading branches of a lime tree. Bees hummed high up in the lime flowers, and chickens pecked and scraped in the earth under the children's feet.

Lo wished she had hair like tiny Sweetpea, who twisted a chestnut brown curl around her fingers and sucked it.

'Now, Pink, it's your turn to read,' said the older girl, who had long dark hair and wore a daisy chain around her brow, like a starry halo.

'*THE BLACK CAT SAT ON THE MAT.*'

'Very good, Pink. And the next line?'

Lo was happy with her new name, unaware that it was the name of a flower, but preferring the colour pink to any other. Her fairyprincessdress had never been returned to her, but she had forgotten it anyway, and enjoyed looking exactly like her new friends in their green shorts and vests. She adored her fifteen-year-old, blue-eyed teacher, whose name was Hazel, and who always wore wild flowers in her hair. Her tinkling laugh made Lo feel safe. Her very own real rabbit had had three babies and she was allowed to keep one of them. She didn't ask what was going to happen to the other two. They lived in a hutch with a big run surrounded by chicken wire with several other small creatures – hamsters and guinea pigs, chickens, ducks, even a young kid. Each of the small girls had a pet among these creatures.

'I had a pussy cat once,' said Sand, clutching a nervous brown hen. Her fine mousy hair was pulled into two plaits tied with green ribbons.

'Did I have one too? asked Lo.

'Don't you remember, Sweetheart?' said Hazel, their young teacher.

'No.' Lo sucked her thumb.

'Did you have a mummy and daddy?' asked Sand. 'I've got lots of mummies now.'

'Course I did...' Lo wasn't sure any more about her past life. She remembered Sid, though, and had for a while after she was taken to Freedom Farm cried herself to sleep thinking about him and wondering why he had gone away.

'I had three Billy Goats Gruff,' she said, smiling confidently at her small audience.

CHAPTER NINETEEN

AT FIRST LIGHT the puppy licked Sid's face and woke him. They had a little Kworn and water and set off again after Sid had relieved himself against the stone hedge. Finding a trickle of water leading to a shallow, tree-shaded stream, Sid filled up the water bottle and washed his sticky face. Izzi sniffed the water suspiciously before drinking his fill and he walked stiff legged, wagging his shaggy tail, ears cocked, through the shallow water. He stood still and moved his head to follow a slight movement on the bottom, pawing at the water every now and then. He made a sudden snap with his teeth and Sid was amazed to see that the dog had caught a small trout.

'Good boy!'

He took the fish from the soft mouth and Izzi started stalking again. Sid joined him, standing still, legs wide, staring into the water. Soon he had four small fish. Sid made a firepit lined with stones, found his matches and made a fire with hairy lichens, dry bracken and dead gorse. He searched for sharp twigs with which to spear the fish. He waited for the smoke to die down and the hot embers to go grey then stuck the ends of the sticks into them. The smell of the cooking fish brought saliva to his mouth. He ate while they were still too hot, so they burned his tongue, but it was still the best food he had ever eaten. He shared it with the hungry puppy, who wolfed it down and put his head on one side for more.

'You're a born hunter, Izzi. We make a good team, you and me.' The dog wagged his tail and gave a low woof. The dog wanted to go back to the stream but Sid called him and he obeyed. He needs company more than he needs food, thought Sid.

Sid set off again to look for Lo, and in the back of his mind was the thought of the daisy girl: her shiny hair, her laugh.

He wasn't sure what he was going to do when he found Lo, except that he wanted to reassure her that he hadn't forgotten her. He wanted to see if she was happy and well or if she wanted to go with him. Where? He didn't know. He ought to go back to Penzance to search for his grandmother – Grumps. That had been his main aim. But what good would it do if he did find her? Would she be prepared to hide a small girl from the Reducers? He had thought about this problem for days and had made a decision – he wouldn't bother to look for her.

On the other hand, if Lo was unhappy, it was his duty to rescue her from the New-Earthers and make sure she was safe. He could look after her himself well enough. They could go back to the roundabout, he supposed, or to the old pig farm, or even the gravel pit lake. He thought of the little boat, the still water with the surrounding trees full of the sound of birdsong, the hovering green and gold dragonflies. Most of all he thought about the boat. Izzi would like it there. The little dog could catch fish for them. They could all swim in the cool water. Could he persuade the daisy girl to go with them? They could live happily ever after.

If only!

'Too much imagination,' his mam had said about him.

They wandered over the moors, lying in the sun or shade, chasing rabbits in tussocky grass. He took a pot shot at a nibbling rabbit about ten metres away. To his delight and horror it lurched over on its side, dead. Izzi ran to collect it and proudly delivered it to Sid.

Recollecting the way the Reducer had prepared the rabbit for them to eat he made slashes at its tail end and peeled back the fur. It was more difficult than it had looked when Mal had done it. He didn't do it cleanly, but he managed to remove most of it. He admired the rabbit's pink shiny skin. Izzi played with the fur, worrying it and growling, licking at the odd bits of flesh that adhered. After throwing the steaming guts to the puppy, Sid dug a shallow firepit, glad he had matches to light a fire, and lined it with flat stones.

Boy and dog ran and played together on the high moor, out of sight of the town and heliport. It was as if only he and Izzi were left in the world. That would be fine, he thought. We could survive together, look after each other. The country was a good place to live, he decided. After a meal of half cooked meat, which was quite disgusting, and made him want to gag, he gave the rest to the dog and zipped up the remaining matches in the waterproof backpack.

But he hadn't extinguished the fire properly and a sudden sharp breeze relit the embers and a spark escaped from the opened firepit. Bracken burst into flame around him. It happened in a flash, before he had time to stamp on all the small flames. Scared, he bolted.

'Come on Izzi, run for it.'

Behind them the moor was alight, smoke rising in a plume as fire nibbled and consumed dry grass, bracken and heather. Small creatures ran, terrified. Larks abandoned their burning nests and eggs. Soon a helicopter throbbed over the blackened land and fire-fighters were sent out to tackle the blaze before it spread as far as the town. Sid could hear the noise behind him as they fled.

After traipsing through a valley of damp bog-land, where they drank at a small dark pool, he reached another barren moor, brown with dead bracken. They stalked a pheasant, and Sid marvelled at the colours of this exotic bird, the golden tail. He wasn't hungry and anyway he thought it was too beautiful to eat, so he made no attempt to shoot it, though it would have been easy for him to do it, the bird was so slow, and flew awkwardly, like a chicken. He thought it might be a peacock, but without a spread tail covered in eyes.

All at once he realised that he could no longer see the sea on either side. He hadn't been concentrating, and now he wasn't sure which way was which.

Low clouds covered the hills and he heard a roll of thunder, like a giant clearing his throat. A flash of lightning came close after, and hail, like cold pebbles, fell on them. They ran across the open moor, over ancient stiles, past flattened cotton-flowers, through boggy places, looking for shelter. There were no trees, only stunted blackthorn leaning away from the interminable south-westerlies.

Soaked and chilled, and concerned that lightning might be attracted to the metal of his rifle, Sid ran towards a small building in the corner of a field, which, when he got closer, he could see was a ruined shed. Maybe it had been an animal shelter, he thought, or a shepherd's hut in the days when there were still herds of sheep and cows and pigs. He thought of the cow they had seen at Zennor, its glamorous eyelashes, the long tongue and hot breath, and wished he had some warm milk now. Ivy grew through the stacked granite blocks, and crows flew off, squawking in disapproval. A small part of slate roof still stood, and he crouched under it; the puppy, pink tongue lolling, shivered close by.

'Good boy, Izzi. Good boy.' Sid held him. 'Don't be frightened. It's only a storm. Maybe your first, eh?' Having the small creature to look after made him feel brave. It was like when he had Lo to care for. It made him forget his own fears. Perhaps that's how his mam and dad had felt about him and Lo, he thought. They had had to pretend nothing bad was going to happen to them, because they didn't want to frighten their children. At that moment he forgave his father for not taking them somewhere safe, away from the Reducers, before it was too late. It was not always easy to have the care of weaker creatures, he realised. Life was simpler when you only had yourself to think about. But he wouldn't be without the dog now he had him. He needed the companionship of the puppy as much as the puppy needed him. This live Izzi was even better than the imaginary Isambard.

Thunder exploded around him, and lightning pierced the moors. Hail turned to drenching rain, eased off a little, and stopped. The air was full of moisture; purple and orange clouds surrounded them.

Water dripped from a yellow kingcup bent horizontal by the force of the storm. The little dog licked at it, tentatively.

'Time to make a run for it, Izzi.'

Sid set off downhill to cross a stream, but the rain started again, heavier than before; the sky blackened and lightning came again, scaring him. He watched as the only tree in sight was lit with a burst of fire and burned up.

'Come on boy.' He lifted the puppy, holding it close and stumbled over the boulder-strewn sea-field to a small stone bridge. There was a stream running fast under it, where it had been dry just a short while ago. Thunder cracked again and lightning came almost instantaneously. The storm was right overhead. He ducked under the bridge and crouched shivering up against the granite pile, holding the puppy close. He thought he was safe there. The bridge was hundreds of years old, he could tell by the lichens and moss that covered the stone. His father would have told him the history of the little granite bridges and the dry stone hedges if he had been here.

But he isn't, is he? thought Sid, and terror seized him as a rushing clattering noise assailed his ears and a flash flood plucked him and the puppy from under the bridge and swept them away. The stream was now a raging river, breaking the mud banks, churning the earth and taking debris – stumps of thorn bushes, gorse, bracken, brambles, boulders even, shifting them as if they were fragile flowers, turning all into a morass, a cauldron of thick brown soup. The force of water twisted the boy and separated him from the dog. He held his breath as he felt the water dragging him under. Black – it was black and cold. He was tumbled over and over, buffeted by rocks and logs. He sensed air for a moment and took another gasp of breath.

A picture came to Sid of Brunel, a small man, with his tall black hat, bizarrely smoking a cigar, being swept along with him in the floodwater. Brunel had survived the tidal wave that broke through the damaged Thames Tunnel, saved by the water, which bore him along the tunnel and up one of the shafts, where his inert body was snatched from the tide. Sid kept that image in his mind. If Brunel could survive, so could he.

At one time Sid thought he touched the puppy, but he wasn't sure. His clothes were shredded from him, the backpack tugged him down. He tried to swim but it was hopeless. His lungs felt like they were about to burst. He was pressed down by the weight of water. He stopped fighting and let the flood take him, down, down.

CHAPTER TWENTY

MAL AND THE REST of Heyl Exterminating Angels had their orders: find the Runners who had an established encampment somewhere in the hills between Zennor and Penzance. Women of childbearing age, concealing Runner kids, and surviving by growing their own food.

Take them out. Reduce them all.

His hip had healed, as had his shoulder and arm, though in wet weather he still ached.

Age, he thought. I'm getting old. Mustn't get old and useless – I'll get reduced. His mates had joked with him about his missing week away from Heyl Reducer HQ.

'Got a woman, eh?'

'Where's she to? Did she nurse you, then?'

He had lost weight and muscle while he was recuperating. He had to try harder to keep up with his mates when they trained. He couldn't run like he used to. Negotiating the bike round corners hurt his shoulder, though he didn't complain. Plenty of others waiting to take his place if he wasn't up to the job.

He thought often of the roundabout kids and wondered if they were still alive, or had they died of hunger, or maybe they'd got sick and there was no one to look after them.

He tried not to think about the little girl – Lo, she was called Lo. And he tried not to remember the other girl child, that first time he had been sent out on a Reduction exercise. Better not to remember, but he couldn't control his dreams. He fought sleep, but when oblivion inevitably swept over him he suffered the same nightmare again and again. Except that it wasn't a nightmare. It was true.

CHAPTER TWENTY-ONE

WHEN MORNING CAME, there were scenes of devastation along the narrow valley. A cottage had been destroyed in the flood, fallen into a torrent that all the locals had known only as a small trickle of water before. Luckily, no one was living there any more – fled the year before, in fear of the Reduction.

Two farmers had a lucky escape when their chimney was struck by lightning and had fallen through the roof. It had gone through a ceiling and crashed onto the empty beds of their daughter and the little grand-daughter they had lost to the flu twelve months before. Mud had washed into kitchen doors, and sewage welled up from drains, and flooded floors. Foul-smelling sofas and armchairs sat in small gardens with spread out carpets. The usually reclusive occupants of the hamlet talked to each other over garden walls. Neighbours helped neighbours to rebuild damaged sheds and shared provisions. The farmers repaired the roof, replanked the wooden ceiling and made the little girl's room as it had been before the storm: a shrine to their lost daughter and grandchild, with dolls, bunk beds, and pretty curtains.

Half a mile away there was a stony beach, where the stream emptied itself into the Atlantic Ocean. Oystercatchers searched for shellfish among the rocks, beaks probing, red legs hurrying. Cormorants dived for small fish. On a large clump of rocks that made up a small island, others stood, stretching out their ragged wings to dry. Hungry gulls complained and squabbled, lifting on the thermals above the granite cliffs.

Waterfalls gushed out of the cliff onto the deserted beach. The sky was the blue of a robin's egg. Sun gilded the wet pebbles. A man came out of a small hut built up against the cliff, and scratched his grey beard. He wore his wispy grey hair in a pony-tail and carried a sack over one shoulder. His shorts (which had once been dark blue but were now an indiscriminate colour), were held up around his waist with blue string. He kept hitching them up to stop them falling over his skinny hips. His dark tanned face and neck were wrinkled with a thousand lines. His muscled legs bore scars and snaking blue veins.

Sniffing the air, he knew that the hot autumn weather had broken at last. He detected burnt bracken, a hint of sewage, and the usual salt-sea aroma of seaweed. He placed buckets under little waterfalls that gushed from the cliff and stooped to gather driftwood. Once the sack was full he made his way easily over the boulders and pebbles to a deep cave where he kept his boat. The cave was dry and the boat still secure where he had hidden it the night before. Then he went round a rocky headland to where the stream emptied onto the shore to see if the flood had brought him anything interesting or useful.

The dog whined and wagged his tail and licked the face of the unconscious boy. He growled and tugged again at the heavy backpack slung around the boy's shoulders.

Sid coughed.

The puppy's barks woke him from a dark place. A man stood over him silhouetted against a deep blue sky. Sound of waves breaking on rocks. Smell of fish and fire. He coughed up water and vomited dirt. His tongue felt thick. The puppy kept on barking. Sid felt himself lifted up and carried. Was aware of the crackle of pebbles rubbing together. He heard gulls calling and thought he was flying. It was a good feeling, exhilarating. He felt safe. Then he drifted back into the dark deep place, where water was all around him and he was helpless.

The man pushed an enamel mug at Sid's lips. The boy coughed and shivered and didn't open his eyes and couldn't drink the hot tea. The man had wrapped him in a blanket, but the boy still shook. The man took the boy in his arms and using the blanket as a towel he rubbed the boy's back and chest hard, and then did the same with his legs and arms. The boy's head lolled. The dog wagged his tail and yapped.

'S'orright, boy, he'll be right as rain soon.'

Izzi sat gazing intently at Sid. The man had fed the dog rabbit meat, which Izzi had eaten enthusiastically. The young dog needed sleep but more, he wanted the boy to be awake and talking to him, fondling him. The boy slept on the plank-wood bed, while the man went about his work, drawing a sketch of the faithful dog, the unconscious boy. He used up nearly all the charcoal. He chose a piece of hardboard from his stack in a corner and opened one of his last tins of paint – thrown up by the sea a year ago. He used the stalk of a deep-sea weed – he hadn't a brush – to spread red paint over the board.

Sid felt warm again, but exhausted, as if he had been on an epic journey, though he was confused about where he had been and where he was now. He ached all over. Izzi yelped with delight and licked the boy's face as he groaned and opened his eyes for the first time. Sid was in a small room that smelt of tar and paint. The sloping roof was made of tin. How did he get here? He could hear the sea shuddering and falling. He coughed and spluttered and brought up phlegm and dirt.

'Orright then, boy?' said the man leaning over him.

'Where am I?' Sid wiped his mouth with his hand.

'My place. You're safe, boy. Nearly drowned, you were.'

'Drowned?'

'Reckon the dog saved you. Some strong he be, for a young dog. Dragged you out of the flood anyway. Found you in rocks, I did.'

'Izzi!' Sid held the large puppy in his arms. He hurt all over but nothing seemed to be broken. He had bruises and minor abrasions on his legs and arms, and large welts where the backpack straps had cut into him. The dog was uninjured. All around him on the floor were buckets and bowls full of water. It still dripped from holes in the roof. The dog pulled away and lapped from one of the buckets.

'Do you remember what happened?'

'I was under a bridge sheltering from the lightning.'

'Flash flood took you, I reckon. Here, have some brew.'

CHAPTER TWENTY-TWO

'THANKS,' HE SAID to the man, who looked and smelt like a tramp but his blue eyes were kind. 'You're an artist!'

The small room was lined with paintings on board; even the planks that made up the walls had paintings on them. They reminded him of the gallery where the North Newlyn Repops were based: sailing boats that looked like gulls, gulls that looked like boats, moonscapes and seascapes in black charcoal, and paintings all in red.

'What's your name, boy?'

'Sid. Sid Kingdom Freeman. Sidney after my mam's father, Kingdom after the engineer.'

The man grinned. 'Big name for a lad. Call me Gaz.'

'Gaz?'

'Short for Gascoigne, but no one ever called me that, except Mother.' He was about sixty, short, wiry and muscled with not one ounce of fat on him. He had a wire ear-ring in one ear, with a cockleshell dangling from it and around his neck he wore a leather string with another cockleshell strung onto it. On his head was a battered seaman's cap with fish hooks stuck in the band. His fisherman's smock was the same faded blue as the sky.

'Not a Runner, are you?'

'Nah, I'm a Repop.' Should he tell the man about Lo? He wasn't sure.

'What's a Repop?'

'Special. Going to Repopulate the planet, when it's time.'

'On your own?'

Sid laughed, coughing up more muck. The man laughed with him and the dog barked and jumped up and down, wagging his tail in excitement.

'Well, Sid Kingdom Freeman, put these on and come with me. Got to get you moving. Warm you up.' The man shoved a faded denim shirt and a pair of paint spattered shorts at Sid. 'Going foraging.' He gave Sid some string to tie the waist of the baggy shorts to stop them slipping down. Sid limped behind Gaz along the shore and onto the rocks at the edge. It was low tide.

'See this clump of mussels? Well, go for the big ones; leave the littl'uns to grow some more. Get the ones without barnacles or weed on, they're easier to clean.'

'They're difficult to get off, aren't they?' Sid tugged at the shellfish that were stuck hard to each other and the rock. The sleeves of the man's shirt were too long for him and he had to keep folding them back, but the action was warming him up.

'Twist the stringy bit and yank them off, like that.'

Sid noticed that Gaz was missing the top of the middle finger on his left hand.

They soon had a bag full of mussels, which Gaz put in a bucket of fresh water, and he showed Sid how to get rid of the byssus, the stringy bit that acted as anchor. Sid's fingers were sore from pulling at them.

'Soon toughen you up, boy, don't you worry.' He showed Sid his red hands, roughened and calloused. Sid wanted his hands to look like that. Tough, lined, wrinkled, like the man's face, full of wisdom, he thought. The dog chased the waving weaving seaweed, barked at gulls always just out of reach on the green granite rocks. The herring gulls, feathers blowing backwards, stared at the yapping dog. Before he reached them they lifted, disdainfully, away from danger.

Gaz put the cleaned bivalves in a pan of water with some added torn up wild onion leaves over a cooking fire on the beach until they opened and were ready to eat.

'Won't the coastguard see the smoke?'

'Don't you worry about they. I've never seen one.' He scooped a mussel up from the hot liquor with his fingers. 'Take the mussel in both hands and pull the shells apart, like so and swallow the meat.'

The mussel meat was yellow and white and looked quite different from anything Sid had eaten before. He tentatively chewed one. It was delicate, not rubbery, and tasted like the sea. He had never tasted anything so good. He watched Gaz use one mussel shell as a spoon and copied him. Companionable and silent except for the slurping noises, they shared the soup from the pan.

'My dog can catch fish. He got three in a pool.' Izzi sat close to the boy, wagging his tail. Sid threw him some mussel meat and the dog wolfed it down.

'That's a rare beast you have there,' he said. 'You're some lucky, you are.'

'He's called Izzi.'

'Is 'e?'

'That's right, Izzi. After Isambard Kingdom Brunel.'

'So, your name Kingdom, is that after Isambard Kingdom Brunel, too?'

The boy nodded proudly, sipping the mussel soup. 'You've heard of him, then?'

'Oh 'es, built the bridge between Devon and Cornwall, over the Tamar. Learned it at school.' The man casually set about making an under-sand fire. He buried a good-sized log deep in a firepit, sitting it on dried seaweed and bracken to get it going.

'Why are you doing that?'

'Making charcoal.'

'Why?'

'Artist, ain't I? Need charcoal to draw.' He smiled. He didn't have many teeth. Sid thought of the man in the train carriage. He hadn't had many teeth either, but he felt that he could trust this man.

Sid told him about the firepit he had had on the roundabout. He also told him about Mal and how he had nursed him.

'Stay away from roads, boy, I do. Stay away from people if I can. Don't trust people, me. Nasty, most of them.'

He spat onto the pebbles.

Sid thought about all the people he had met on his journeys: Mal, who had shot a rabbit and cooked it for them, but was a killer; the one-eyed man in the train carriage who had taken his knife but had told him where the New-Earthers had taken Lo.

The flick-knife! And the rifle. Where were they? He must have lost them in the flash flood.

He thought about the Repops, his friend Buzz, who had not let him down; Rook, who had been nice to him at first, but had told the military leaders about his photo. It was Rook who had told the other lads to kill the puppy. It was difficult to tell who was a good person and who wasn't, he thought. People seem to have both good and bad inside them. And he remembered with a pang of guilt, how, when he had the rifle, he had shot at the women in the field, to scare them, just because he was angry with them. They hadn't done anything wrong, only mocked him. He was like everyone else, he thought sadly, bad when he had power over someone, nice when he needed them.

When the charcoal was made, Gaz even let him try his hand at drawing. Sid drew a picture of Izzi and another of the man.

'I never look like that, do I?'

'What's wrong with it?'

'But I'm old! What will the ladies think? Better shave off my beard.' The man laughed and propped the picture up against the wall with all the others.

'Why are all these paintings red, Gaz?'

'Bleddy geet tin of red oxide thrown up on the beach, last year, I think it was. Good for them sunsets.'

A couple of days later, while Sid was sheltering in the cave from the cold easterly wind that had blown up, he spotted his rifle on a high shelf of rock. He supposed that it had washed down onto the beach in the flood and Gaz had found it.

'That's my rifle in the cave,' he told the man when he saw him.

'Finders keepers,' said Gaz.

'But, it's mine, I lost it when I was swept away.'

'So what? Mine now, boy.'

'Didn't find my flick-knife, did you?' Strangely, Sid wasn't put out by the idea that his weapons had been confiscated by Gaz. It felt good to have someone he trusted take charge.

The man shook his head, disapprovingly. 'What d'you want with a flick-knife?'

He rummaged around in the shack and came out with a steel-bladed knife with a bone handle. 'Here, you can have this if you like.'

'Oh, it's ace! Thanks, Gaz.'

He spent the afternoon whittling himself a stave from an old broom handle he had found on the tide line. He rather missed the Repop lance. Was Buzz still alive, he wondered, and if so, did he appreciate the sacrifice that Sid had made? The new lance wasn't as long or heavy as the old one, he thought – or maybe he was stronger now, and taller.

'Ain't you better be getting back to they there Repops, then?'

'Do you want me to go?' He tried not to sound anxious, but more than anything he wanted to stay here on the beach with the man.

'Do what you want, boy, don't worry me. Stay as long as you like.'

Sid still hadn't mentioned Lo. He knew that he would have to make a decision sometime. Was he going to fetch her, or leave her where she was with the women?

'Anyway, can't go back. No dogs allowed in Repops. They'd reduce him.'

He threw a stone into the waves and Izzi chased it joyfully, nuzzling the water and wagging his tail.

They went out on a foraging trip for more wild food. Gaz carried Sid's rifle and a sack.

'No harm in you learning how to find food in the countryside,' Gaz said, picking at a clump of pennywort that was growing from a dry-stone hedge. 'Just the penny- shaped leaves, see, not the yellow flowers.'

'How do you cook them, Gaz?'

The man chewed a few leaves. 'Eat 'em raw, like. Taste.'

Sid plucked a few for himself and chewed tentatively. Gaz carried on searching the length of the ancient wall between two fields.

'See this? Ivy-leaved toadflax, it is.' He ate a few leaves. 'Not bad, eh?'

As they walked they gathered whatever Gaz identified as being edible – young nettles, which he grabbed firmly so as not to get stung; young alexanders, which he said he would fry up if he had some butter, but as they hadn't any, he would put them in a soup with the nettles. He plucked a bunch of gorse flowers, not bothered about the thorns. Sid winced as he tried to do the same thing. The mustard coloured flowers had a coconut scent to them.

'What will you do with those?'

'Make a fine tea, they do, you'll see.'

Izzi sniffed the air and growled softly. Gaz thrust the sack into Sid's hands and told him to be quiet. At the edge of the sea-field sat a hare, tall ears twitching. One shot and it was lying on its side.

'Fetch!' he told the dog, who raced over to the dead hare and carried it back in his soft mouth, dropping it at Gaz's feet. Gaz skinned it straight away, throwing the guts to the dog, who sniffed then gobbled the still steaming offal, his tail wagging in joy. The man put the pelt and the meat into his sack.

In the far field, the doe slunk away, alone now and uncomprehending.

On the way back they walked through the small hamlet on the bluff and were seen by a tall farmer woman peering at them over a granite wall. She half raised an arm in greeting, but Gaz ignored it.

'Why don't we get food from the farm?' Sid asked, perplexed at the man's obvious hostility.

'Don't choose to be beholden to anybody.'

Sid remembered the home-cooked food he and Lo had had from the Zennor woman, and regretted the man's independence.

Back at the beach, Gaz bruised the gorse flowers by rubbing them in his hands and then threw them into a pot of boiling water.

'Should have honey in it to make it sweeter,' he said, sipping from a tin mug. But Sid thought the drink very tasty. He wished he'd known about wild food when he was living on the roundabout.

Gaz had stripped off two steaks from each side of the hare's spine. The legs were laid with the steaks on top of a grill across the fire. They crouched together and enjoyed the cooking smells, man, boy and dog, in the setting sun. The pelt was curing close by, high up on a string, like a piece of washing, so that Izzi wouldn't be tempted to eat it.

'Don't waste anything,' Gaz remarked. Never know when it will come in useful.' Behind the hut was a pile of found things that 'might come in useful': an odd rubber flip-flop, rolls of wire, old fishing nets, fish boxes, plastic bottles, anything that the tide carried in and left on his doorstep.

'I suppose I better be going soon,' said Sid, regret in his voice. Izzi was paddling in the shallow pools, scrabbling with his paws and biting at floating weed and scuttling crabs.

'Where are you going, then?'

'To find my little sister.'

'Lost is she?'

'No, not lost, but...'

'Don't tell us if you don't want to, boy.'

'No, I do want to tell you. She's with some New-Earthers, only I've forgotten where they are.'

'They women what don't allow men in their camp?'

'Yes, them.'

'They'll look after her, don't you fret. I'll show you where they're to if you like. Take them shellfish sometimes, I do, in return for chicken eggs and other things.'

'You know where they are? Freedom Farm it's called.'

'Freedom's not far. In a hidden valley, it is.'

'That's it. With nut trees and caravans and tents and stuff.' Sid fell over the words, he was so excited.

'Then what are you going to do? Won't let *you* in, will they?'

'I want to make sure she's okay, safe. I don't know what I'll do then. If she wants to go with me, maybe we'll make it back to a den we had once. There was fresh water there.' He sounded sad. 'I was going to find my grandfather but he's dead and Gran – Grumps – doesn't like children.'

The man made himself comfortable on a flat rock by the fire. They sat together, mesmerised by the sight and sound of green waves crashing a few metres away onto the half sand, half pebble shore.

'Bring her here if you want. Live along with me.'

'Really? Really?' Sid squeaked. It was too good to be true. 'What about my dog?'

'He's a good'un. Don't mind him either.'

'But you've no room for us really.' Gaz had been sleeping on the floor, Izzi on the bed with Sid.

'No problem, boy, I'll build on another room.'

'Can I help?' Sid couldn't believe the man's generosity. Lo would love to live on the beach with a dog.

'If you like.' The man took Sid to the cave, where as well as the boat, there was a stack of seaborne timber.

'Is this your boat?'

Gaz nodded.

'Can I... do you sail it?' He was aware that there were supposed to be no privately owned boats any more, and wondered if Gaz knew that.

'We'll go out in a day or two if you like, when the sea's calmed down. The storm churned things up.'

They dragged and carried the timber to the hut and began to build.

'What are you going to use as a roof?'

'Got a bit more galvanised left; it'll do us fine.'

When he had finished fixing the roof, Gaz told Sid to gather some furze to camouflage it. It took the boy ages to cut the spiny gorse branches and drag them to the hut, his hands and arms pricked and bleeding. Gaz's hands were like leather, nothing hurt them.

'Now find a few big flat stones to pile on top. Stop it all blowing away in the wind.'

Sid admired Gaz. He could shoot, sew clothes, cook on an open fire in the rocks, paint, and make things from nothing, things like tools and baskets. He made crab pots from willow twigs, which he wet and wove into shape, and constructed wire snares for rabbits, though Sid disapproved of those. Gaz could do anything, even with a missing finger. Sid watched and learned.

'When can we go and find my sister?' he asked Gaz, who was mending a tear in the boat's sail with a thick bent needle and twine, 'now there's somewhere for her to sleep.' He swept the new room clear of sand each morning, feeling proud that he had helped to build something so sturdy.

'We'll go dreckly, when I've got enough stuff to take the women, all right?'

Over the next few days Gaz took him up to the cliff top and showed him how to dowse with a Y-shaped stick to find hidden water wells in the ground. Sid was delighted when the stick moved of its own accord, twisting in his hands.

'You'm a natural, you are, my handsome!' Gaz clapped Sid on the back and the boy's smile widened. 'We don't need any fresh water yet, but when we do I'll know where to find it.'

'Izzi drinks more than we do,' said Sid, watching the spaniel lap rainwater from a bucket. A gull glided past them. 'What about gull eggs? Can we eat them?'

'Can do, but they only lay eggs in the spring, boy, not this time of year.'

They dug a fresh latrine well away from the hut at the other end of the beach, but above the tide line. Gaz leaned on his spade, looking out at the sea.

'We needs a break from digging. Come on, I'll show you how to sail.'

'It's a bit rough, isn't it?'

'It's calm enough.'

It didn't look very calm to Sid: rollers broke on the shore, sucking pebbles into the sea and throwing them back again. Dark swells rose and fell, blurring the horizon. But no waves broke over the distant rocky islet where shag and cormorant stood and preened. There, the sea rose and fell, lapping at the masses of purple mussels that colonised the rock.

It was a clinker built wooden boat, five metres long, with a name painted in red on the stern and side – *Girl Rose*.

'Won't someone see?'

'Who's to see?' The man grinned.

'Coastguards?'

'You seen any?'

'No, but... what about the helicopters?'

'They don't bother with this coast. Too rough, too hazardous, no refugees are going to try and land hereabouts. Where would they come from? America?' Gaz laughed loudly at his own joke, until he started coughing.

The sun was dropping into the waves as they dragged the boat across the beach on wooden poles that acted as wheels. Izzi barked and ran up and down the beach.

'No, Izzi, you have to wait here for us,' said Sid.

'Come if he wants,' said Gaz, and Izzi, as if he been waiting for an invitation, jumped into the boat.

'Get in, boy,' Gaz told Sid, and pushing the boat into the waves he shoved it off, climbing over the side as it floated free. The boat rocked alarmingly and Sid held onto the side.

Gaz dropped the centreplate, hauled up the brown canvas lugsail and fitted the rudder and tiller over the stern. Wind filled the sail and they were sailing. It was the most exhilarating feeling that Sid had ever had, better than leaping from roof to roof, better than fighting with lances. It was like flying. He threw back his head and laughed. They sailed over big waves and into the deep troughs, where the land was invisible to them. They sailed out by the rocks and Sid saw dark heavy creatures flop from the rocks and plunge, then stick doggy heads out of the water, whiskers dripping diamonds.

'What are they?'

'Seals, boy, ain't you never seen a seal?'

Izzi had been standing with his front paws up on the side of the boat, but when he saw the seals he leapt into the water.

'Come back, Izzi, come here.' It was deep water and Sid was scared the pup would drown.

'He's all right. Like to swim, they dogs do.' They watched as Izzi swam after a seal and as the seal dived, Izzi swam in a circle yapping and wagging his tail like a rudder, looking to see where the seal had gone. The seal surfaced some way away, looking towards the dog as if he was calling him to play. Dog and seal played hide-

and-seek for some time, the boy and man watching them. The seal grew tired of the game and dived, not to come up near the dog again. Bewildered, Izzi barked and searched for the seal for a while before heading back to the beach to shake himself and sit on the rock watching the faraway boat.

'Going to try for some fish now,' said Gaz, 'when they seals is far enough away. Steal our catch otherwise.'

They sailed in silence for a while, following the coastline westwards. All that remained of the setting sun was a swathe of fiery clouds. The waves were tinged with pink and yellow. Tall granite chimney stacks rose from the rocks like grey fingers pointing to Heaven.

'What are they?' Sid pointed.

'Old engine houses, for the tin mines,' Gaz replied. 'There were shafts going under the sea years ago. Once, there were thirty-odd men killed when a shaft collapsed. Dangerous work it were. Another time, fifty men or more were drowned underground. Waterspout in the shaft.'

'Like the Thames Tunnel. Isambard Kingdom Brunel was nearly killed when it collapsed,' Sid said, proud of his knowledge.

The man grunted. 'My old feyther told me, follow the seabirds,' he said. 'They know more than we. Watch for gannets diving. Only for garfish, sprats and sand-eel, but it's all you get these days. Big fish all gone, all dead and gone. Used to be mackerel and pilchard years ago, and bigger fish, mullet and bass,' he said. 'Never saw them myself. All dead and gone. Only tiddlers and spider crabs – bleddy ugly critters – no meat on 'em to speak of. Make good soup, though.'

But there were no gannets diving, no gulls hovering. The man's voice was hypnotic; he talked with a lovely sing-song West Cornwall softness. Sid had to listen carefully to understand what he was saying. Not like the harder East Cornish of his father and mother. His poor father and mother! Sid hadn't thought of them for ages. It was as if they were from another time, a different world. He wiped his eyes on his sleeve and sniffed hard.

Gaz sailed the boat to where he had placed a buoy made of an old plastic oil-can. He hauled up a length of chain with a crab pot at the end and found two spider crabs, their long red legs tangled together.

'Take them out, then,' he said, and Sid grabbed the crabs. They had puny claws and he wasn't scared of being pinched.

'Stick them upside down in the bilge.'

'Bilge?'

'Bottom of the boat, boy.'

The crabs lay helpless on their backs, scrabbling the air. They looked like giant scarlet spiders.

'Used to catch bleddy great lobsters, one time. Geet claws on 'em, could take your finger off.' Gaz laughed a rasping laugh and coughed, spitting to leeward.

'Is that how you lost your finger, Gaz?'

'It was, 'es, that's how I lost it, not concentrating. Own fault. Got to watch out when you're dealing with they.'

Gaz rebaited the pot with open mussels and chucked it back over the side into the sea.

Each morning when he woke Sid filled his lungs with the clean salt air. He spent his days running on the beach with Izzi, and incidentally, learning about the beach life around him – which rock plants and seaweeds were good to eat and which were not. There was a rock samphire that Gaz particularly enjoyed. Sid climbed the rock face to gather it for him, glad to be of use. He watched Gaz wash the bunch of pale green succulents in fresh water to get rid of the saltiness, then steam it all over a pan of water. Like the mussels it smelt of the sea. They bit off the fleshy parts, leaving the woody stalks.

'Used to have butter and pepper with these, in the good old days,' Gaz reminisced.

One hot day they were out in the boat, Izzi standing on the bow, his nose pointing up to sniff the air.

'Right, boy, your turn. Move over here, then, carefully now, sit here, that's right. Hold the tiller firmly, but feel the wind talking to you, feel the sea carrying you.'

Sid took the helm and held the rope that was attached to the sail, loving the tug of it, loving the pull of the wind.

'That's it, you're a natural, you are.' Gas pretended to doze while Sid sailed, but when he looked like getting into trouble, he was there in a flash to help get the boat back on course, and to tack the boat against the wind and turn it about.

'Why doesn't it go in a straight line?'

'Have to go to the side of the wind, work with it, not agin it.' Zig-zag, that's the way, zig-zag.' Gaz let Sid sail the boat for half an hour or more. Then he said, 'Move over, I'll show you how to survive a capsize, all right?'

He steered the boat into the quieter waters of a small cove and performed a deliberate gybe and capsize.

As they'd floated in the calm water, the boom and sail floating alongside the hull of the boat, Gaz told him to swim around to the stern, to avoid swimming over the mast, sail and lines. Izzi woofed happily and swam around looking for seals.

'Push down the centreboard,' Gaz told Sid, but he wasn't strong enough.

'Okay, so grab the end of it and pull down. Put your feet on the underwater part of the hull.'

It still lay in the water. Sid's efforts weren't good enough and he was tiring.

'You help,' he begged.

'No, you can do it, son. Climb onto the centreboard and stand on the end of it. Pull the boat up.'

Sid scrambled up and did as Gaz told him, and it worked. He clambered over the side of the now upright dinghy.

'You did it, see!' The man climbed over the side of the boat and bailed out the water. Sid was proud of himself. 'And never leave your boat to rescue anyone. It's your only hope of survival. Never leave your boat.'

Sid was tanned and filling out. He felt like he had lived on the beach all his life. He swam in the surf and let the waves carry him in on his belly. He discovered rock pools exposed at low tides and marvelled at the red jelly-like sea anemones that stretched out sticky tentacles when the water covered them; blennies and shrimp, tiny white crabs and starfish. He learned how to knock limpets off the rocks and eat them raw.

'Can I go sail the boat on my own, Gaz?' He was keen to do it by himself.

'Dreckly, perhaps.'

Izzi paddled in the shallows, tail wagging, watching for movement on the pebbles, scrabbling with his paws at small crabs. Sid made narrow channels in the sand; he dammed the flow and made elaborate bridges from sticks and pebbles. For a time he could forget what he had been through: the terror when his parents were taken away; escaping from the jeep; the flight from the city with Lo; the roundabout den; his fear of the injured Reducer. And the loss of Lo.

One morning, when he had walked to the next cove, foraging for young alexanders and nettles, he heard a mournful wailing, like an overtired Lo when she was a baby. He looked around, holding his breath, listening carefully. It came from out at sea. Izzi sat up straight, his ears pricked, facing the ocean.

'What is it, Izzi? Can you hear a baby, too?' He stroked the dog's head. The sound came from a rock about twenty metres offshore.

'Need binoculars, don't I?' He concentrated hard on the mound of jagged green granite that grew bigger and smaller in the swell. Then he saw, well camouflaged, a mother seal on the fringe of the rock, her young seal wallowing below her in the water. She was singing to it. Or it was singing to her. And the sound and sight moved the boy. He sat on the bank, dropped his head into his hands and sobbed. The dog lay down beside him, head on paws, whining, wagging his tail uncertainly, and gazing unhappily at his boy.

CHAPTER TWENTY-THREE

GAZ WAS USED to having the boy with him, and wasn't relishing the thought of having a small child to care for. But he had promised.

'I reckon it's time to go and fetch your little sister,' he said. They were sat on the beach, backs against a rock watching, as they always did, as the sun set into a pink and purple sea. 'Need more eggs and greens from the women, anyway,' said Gaz.

Sid wore one of Gaz's old pair of shorts, which were huge on him, but Gaz had shortened them, sewing being one of his many talents. He had lent Sid his only other T-shirt. It was tattered and misshapen and had once been red, but was now a very washed out pink. There was a faded message on it – **My parents went to Scilly, and all I got was this T-shirt.** But mostly Sid went bare-backed, bare-foot.

'Have you been to Scilly, Gaz?'

'Years ago. Sailed there I did.'

'What's it like?'

'Perfect,' Gaz said, smiling. 'Perfect.'

'How is it perfect?'

'Clear waters, strange birds and plants you never saw in your life before, dolphins, white sand, safe 'arbours.'

'Is it still like that? Thought it was all gone in the rising oceans?'

'Dunno, boy, went there when I were a nipper. But I did hear that they'd all gone under the water apart from the highest – St Mary's. And that's smaller than it used to be.

'Sailed there on your own?'

'Nah, only part way. It were a race, a boat race like. Gig boats, teams of us, rowing we were.'

'What's gigs?'

'Lifeboats, originally. Thirty-two feet long and a beam of four feet ten inches. Pilots they were. Used to race to incoming fishing boats. To get the work of carrying fish baskets to shore, see? Six oars.'

'Did you win?'

'Nah, had a good time though.' He laughed at his memories. 'They gig girls were some strong. Arm wrestle you stupid then drink you under the table, they could.' Gaz scratched his crotch thoughtfully.

They packed a sack with fresh mussels, spider crabs, rock samphire, several garfish caught that morning, all wrapped in wet seaweed to keep them fresh, and pretty pebbles.

'Women like pretty things.'

Sid had an idea. He went to the far end of the beach where he had seen fragments of green and blue sea-smoothed glass, and gathered a pocketful. He was amused to see Gaz trim his beard, using a piece of broken mirror to see himself. The man showered under a makeshift shower – a bucket of water on a rope – and changed into clean shorts and brightly patterned Hawaiian shirt. He looked ten years younger.

It was a fine morning. The sun hung in front of them as they climbed up the stony valley, following the stream that had carried Sid and his dog to Gaz several weeks ago. The old bridge had been swept away; only a buttress end still stood. Boulders were strewn along the banks. The rocks had already been colonised by new shoots of brambles and tightly coiled ferns. Sid had the horrors as he saw the place where he had been hurled into the raging flood. It all came back: the black water; not being able to breathe; the helpless swirling under the surface; the terrible, irrevocable force of floodwater. He patted the dog's head and turned away. Izzi whined softly and licked Sid's hand.

'IKB and me, we both survived floods,' he whispered proudly to himself.

They passed the cottages, which had been patched up and scrubbed clean of the contaminating waters. No one was about, though washing blew on a line – faded blue sheets, pillowcases, cotton trousers and women's underwear. Sid thought he saw the slight twitch of a curtain at a window. Behind the cottages were several fields planted with potatoes and other vegetables.

'Can't we get stuff from the farmer?' he asked.

'Never goin' to ask 'im for nowt,' Gaz said, and spat, his brow furrowing.

'Why not?'

A grunt was all the answer Sid could get. Gaz took him along a narrow lane bordered by three-foot thick dry-stone hedges, where succulents grew from the cracks and lizards basked in the sun, and off onto the sea-fields, where the dog ran and the boy ran after him. Daisies danced in the wind and Sid wondered if he would see the daisy girl.

A peregrine falcon mewed, and fell like a bullet. Its killer beak stabbed a kit – a young rabbit whose last moments had been carefree, belly full, teeth emerald with succulent grass. A trail of gulls sailed westward across the narrow peninsula. They headed up and over the top of a craggy hill, where nothing grew on blackened scrubby earth and there was the acrid smell of stale fire. The young dog's nose twitched. He ran after imaginary rabbits.

They came at last to a hillside where Sid recognised the valley of densely planted trees below. Boulders shoved up elbows from the ground and Sid thought of his days working with the Repops, clearing stones. He wondered again if Buzz was better now or had he been reduced because he was no longer of any use?

'You going to find your sister, then?'

'Yeah, reckon.'

'You'll have to slip in when the women aren't looking, or they'll have your guts for garters.'

'What's garters?'

'Forget,' Gaz said, grinning.

He rang a bell at the gate. It was made of hollow bamboo slices hung up close together, so that when you pulled a string they clanged like a bell.

Sid hid behind a tree trunk with the dog, praying that he wouldn't bark. Gaz rang the bell again, longer this time. They waited. A small plump woman appeared, a deep red birthmark on one side of her face like a full-blown rose. Sid remembered her: her initial brusqueness and then her kindness and generosity. She had given him wonderful food. His mouth watered at the memory. She had called him 'Son'. Gaz was talking to her and showing her the contents of the sack. He beckoned and Sid came out from his hiding place.

'Hello, you again?' she said, not unkindly. 'Come to see your little sister?' She showed the palm of her hand to Izzi, who sniffed then licked it, wagging his tail.

'Yes, please.'

'Wait here then, both of you.' She went away, carrying the sack of seafood.

Izzi could smell chickens and rabbits and other delicious scents close by. He whined excitedly. Gaz and Sid smelled biscuits and bread and scones baking.

The woman reappeared about ten minutes later, by which time the dog was dribbling and man and boy were almost beside themselves with anticipation, Gaz of fresh cooked meat and green stuff, and Sid because he was desperate to see Lo; a longing for his own flesh and blood.

He didn't recognise her immediately. She had filled out, for a start, and her hair was cut short and fluffy. Also, she was smiling, and he had only remembered her scared look, a frowning little face trying to be brave.

'Sid, Sid, is it really you?'

She sounded so grown-up.

She leaped into his arms and he tried not to let her see his tears.

'Is he your dog? What's he called? I have a real rabbit called Wabbit.'

'Izzi, he's called Izzi.' The dog licked the little girl's hand and wagged his tail. She hugged him.

'He's lovverly. Where'd you find him?'

'We'll leave you to chat for a few minutes, shall we?' The woman led Gaz away into the trees.

'I'm sure they've got lots to say to each other,' she said, as Gaz put his arm around the woman's shoulder and she put her arm around his hips.

'My name's Pink, isn't it lovverly?'

Sid grinned. 'Pink?' He lifted his little sister up and twirled her around, like he used to do when they were at home with their parents. In the garden with the swing. 'Miss me, Lo? Pink?'

She gave him a soggy kiss on the cheek and laughed. 'We got reading later.'

'Reading, eh? What are you reading?'

'Dunno, books. They got books here. Why don't you stay, Sid?'

'Wouldn't you like to come with me?'

'Where?'

'To live on the beach.'

She frowned. 'I like it here, Sid. Can't you stay?'

'Nah, not allowed, am I?'

'But I want you to meet my fwends.' She had slipped back to baby talk. 'Please, Sid.'

'Is there a girl with daisies in her hair? Long dark hair?'

'She's not a girl. She's my teacher.'

'What's her name, then?'

'Hazel.'

'Hazel.' He tasted the unusual name. Like the nuts, he thought. Like the tree. Hazel. He felt a slipping in his stomach, a surge of excitement. He had her name now. He could hear the distant laughter of women. Drawing his sister into the shade of a tree he asked, 'Are you happy here, is she kind to you?'

'Everybody's kind here.'

The man and woman reappeared from the bushes.

'Best be off, boy. Eh? You coming?'

'Lo, are you sure you want to stay here? Don't you want to be with me?'

'I want to stay here,' she said firmly. 'You can visit me when you like.'

'Okay, Gaz, I'm coming. I'll be back to visit you when I can, Lo.' He kissed the little face. 'Be good, be safe.' He stroked her hair. Remembering the coloured glass, he gave it to her.

'Give a few little bits to Hazel, from me, eh? Tell her thanks for looking after you.'

Gaz kissed the woman's rose-coloured cheek and slapped her on the backside.

'Ooh, you devil, get on with you,' she said, laughing. She hitched Lo up onto her broad hip. The little girl clung, wrapping her legs around the woman, and waved happily to her brother. A breeze sang in the trees.

Man, boy and dog set off again up the hill, the sun to their left. Swallows strafed the meadow, skimming the grass. Sid took the sack from Gaz, who was coughing badly and couldn't catch his breath. He was coughing a lot lately, Sid thought.

'Orright, Gaz?'

'Spot of hay fever, is all.' Gaz spat a jet of phlegm. 'Give me some cloth to make you a decent pair of shorts, she has. Honey, chicken, tatties, greens. Live like lords, we will.'

Sid was quiet on the journey back, carrying the sack most of the way. He wished he had been able to catch a glimpse of the girl – Hazel. Hazel – her name had a 'z' in it. Like Izzi, and Gaz, like Penzance where his grandmother lived. All the significant names in his life had 'z' in them. Marazion where Lo was kidnapped. Zennor where they slept in the church with the mermaid carved on the seat, and the woman had fed them. Brunel's first name could have been spelt with a 'z' instead of an 's', he thought. And he realised that he had stopped worrying about Lo. The nagging ache of anxiety had dissipated, had blown away on the wind. She was obviously settled and well-cared for with the New-Earthers. He would give up the idea of trying to find their grandmother.

CHAPTER TWENTY-FOUR

I LIKE WABBIT
I LIKE CHICKS
I LIKE NUTS
I LIKE SID
I LIKE HAZEL
I LIKE DONKEY

LO SUCKED HER THUMB and thought of what else she liked. She raised her arm.

'Hazel, how do you spell Angels?'

The children had sheets of rough grey paper and sticks of charcoal. They sat in a half circle around their youthful teacher, who hummed quietly to herself and twirled a lock of soft brown hair around her fingers.

Chickens crept pecking at the dry earth between the feet of the children. The donkey brayed loudly in the distance, a terrible, peace-destroying sound, which was half hilarious, half terrifying. As if it was made by an alien creature. What was it trying to convey? Hunger, disappointment, boredom, a warning, or simply a need to be heard and acknowledged? Sid wondered what is must be like to be a donkey.

He had hidden himself on the fork of a tree, above where the children had lessons. There was a canvas awning strung between branches to keep rain and bees away from the children, and he couldn't see much, but he could see Hazel. Happiness filled his heart.

Gaz had taken Izzi out in the boat. The dog had become adept at herding fish towards his nets and the man was delighted with him. Sid had ostensibly gone to gather furze for their cooking fire, and he took the opportunity to go back to Freedom Farm, drawn there by the need to see, not only his little sister, but the girl with dark hair – Hazel.

'Hazel, I want a wee-wee,' said Lo, putting up her arm.

'Go on then, be quick.' Hazel clapped her hands and Lo ran off towards the latrines.

The girl's head was crowned with a circlet of daisies, as before. He could almost smell her faint flowery scent, or so he imagined. Her soft voice rose and fell and he leaned against the tree trunk listening in pleasure to her sudden laughter.

The bees buzzed around him in and out of the ivy flowers, adding to their golden burden of pollen. (On his way here he had seen old-fashioned straw skeps – beehives hidden under a hedge, the occupants dancing and droning above and around). But the buzzing became louder and he thought maybe a helicopter was coming. He looked up but all he could see were the creamy flowers and leathery leaves, the dark boughs and trunk of the lime tree. He heard the hum of bees in his ears, the humming of the girl. Then the louder, harsher note of motorbikes revving through the trees, and the frightened shouts of women. The children looked to Hazel, who was frozen for a moment, her mouth open in a silent scream.

'Run! Run! The hole, the hole!' The children disappeared like mice, faster than thought. Sid shifted slightly so he was jammed up against the tree trunk, his heart beating fast. The awning hid most of the action from him, and he couldn't see where they had gone.

Mal was first on the scene. He rode through the narrow entrance into the nut grove and right to the centre of the camp. Women ran in every direction, as did chickens and ducks. The piglet ran out of the open gate and up the hill as fast as his short legs could carry him, squealing loudly. From out of a shed came a small girl, blonde, fluffy-haired, singing loudly to herself. He removed his helmet. She stood for a moment and stared at him.

'Angel!' she whispered. He replaced his helmet, pulled down the visor, revved the motorbike towards her, snatched her up with one arm and drove into the trees.

Sid heard shots, screams, the whistle and crack of gunfire and saw the flash of flame from a gun. Rooks flapped out of the tall trees, complaining loudly, and fled in a black cloud away from the mayhem. The donkey bolted, splattering excreta in a zigzag trail behind her. Chickens flapped and squawked in distress. Nineteen motorbikes screeched to a halt in a circle under the lime tree.

'Okay, got 'em all, I think. Finish the donkey off – effin' racket – and take the rest of the livestock – we'll have a right feast later. Goat curry, yeah? Hog roast? It was a Reducer with horns on his helmet and the name Dreg in metal studs on the back of his leather jacket. 'There you are, mate. Missed all the fun, as usual.'

The biker he spoke to had a bee buzzing around his face. He removed his helmet and revealed the tattoo of an angel on his bald head. Waving his arms about, he looked up and saw Sid's terrified face.

'Come on Dreg,' the latecomer said. 'Let's get out of here. Bleddy bees everywhere.'

'Fire the vans and tents first,' Dreg ordered. They started up their motorbikes and raced off.

Sid felt sick. By not giving him away the Reducer had saved his life. But what about Lo and the other children? Hazel? Had they all been killed?

He became aware of the smell of smoke, the crackle of fire. He slid down from the tree, and ran first to one shack, then another. The yurt was an inferno, the tents burnt to the ground. A pall of smoke hung like a sea-fret in the trees.

'Lo, Lo! he yelled. No answer. His throat felt tight, his mouth dry. He was shaking, coughing.

He crept slowly through the camp looking for signs of life, frightened that he would find someone injured and be unable to help. They lay where they had been working – a woman slumped over a wheelbarrow, the body of another on a smouldering cooking fire. He tried not to look. He tried to hold his breath so he did not have to smell burning flesh, but it was useless, his throat and nostrils were full of the stench.

He called out again, 'Lo, Lo, are you there? Where are you?' He counted eight dead women and three older girls – not Hazel – but could see no little children. What was it that Hazel had said? The hole, the hole! What hole?

He looked inside the only shack still standing. Gaz's friend looked peacefully asleep at a table, where she had been shelling peas. Scattered peas were all around her on the floor, a neat bullet hole in the middle of her forehead.

He staggered out and vomited. He went next to a wrecked caravan where he had seen Hazel washing her hair that time – it seemed years ago. The blackened door swung on a hinge. There was no one inside. But then he heard something shift, a creak, a whispering under his feet. He grabbed at a trap door and wrenched it up. And there they were – Hazel, eyes wide with fear, and hidden behind her, the little girls, sobbing, terrified.

He lifted them out. The children, their faces black from smoke, had wet themselves in fear. They clung to the legs of the older girl, whimpering.

'Where's Lo?' He didn't recognise his own voice – a harsh croak like a sick crow.

'Lo? Do you mean Pink? Are you Sid? She's told me about you.'

'Where is she?' He spoke quietly, trying to control his trembling voice.

'She went to the latrine. I don't know.' Hazel was trying not to break down.

'Show me.' He grabbed her arm and thrust her forward, and the children moved with her as if they were glued to her limbs.

Hazel screamed, 'Don't look, don't look,' to the children, as they passed smouldering and bloody corpses. The little girls shove their faces into her legs, and clung to her.

There was no body at the burnt-out latrines.

'Lo, Lo, where are you?' Sid yelled. He heard a sob and saw

her high on the horizontal branch of a tree, almost invisible in the deep shadows.

'Hold on Lo.' He climbed up and hauled her down with difficulty as in her fear and shock she hung on and wouldn't let go.

'How did you get up there?' he asked her, holding her tight.

'The angel put me there. He told me to stay and I'd be safe.'

Hazel sobbed and laughed and patted Lo's head.

'The angel?'

'You wemember the angel, Sid?'

'Yes, I remember the angel.'

He said to Hazel, 'Come on, I'll take you somewhere safe.'

'What shall I do? The children! Is there no one else alive…? My mother?' She sobbed and pulled at her hair. The daisy crown was no more.

'Come or stay, it's up to you, but they might be back.'

'I must find her.'

They ran through the camp, until Hazel fell on the body of one of the women. It was Moth. She sobbed and kissed the dead woman's cheek. The little ones were silent now with shock.

'We must bury the dead,' she said.

'No, the Reducers might come back.'

He waited while they quickly gathered together some treasures – blankets, dolls, books. Lo couldn't find the rabbits and all the girls were heartbroken about the dead donkey. The rest of the livestock had gone. A robin sang somewhere, and a breeze shifted the branches, sending the scent of apples to mix confusingly with the acrid and sickening smell of fire and death.

'We're going to the seaside,' Sid said, lifting Lo onto his back and the taking the tearful little girls by their hands.

'The seaside!' whispered Lo.

CHAPTER TWENTY-FIVE

GAZ CAUGHT A big pollock, the first in weeks. It would make a good fish stew with a few sea-leeks and onions thrown in, sea-carrot and sea-kale. He really should think of growing his own vegetables above the beach, but not doing so gave him a good excuse to visit the women, his woman, Rose. He sailed back to the shore, the dog swimming by the side of the boat. But when he got to the shore, instead of shaking himself and rolling in the sand, Izzi ran off barking.

'Must be the boy coming home,' he said to himself, and an unexpected pang of grief hit him. His nine-year-old son, Mathew – his and Rose's boy – had died in the cow flu seven years ago. Rose had joined the Freedom Women's Camp in the aftermath of her grief, and coincidentally, when the Population Control Program began.

'Where are you taking us?' Hazel asked.

'Somewhere where you'll be safe.'

'Nowhere's safe,' she cried, as two helicopters roared towards them and Sid dragged his brood into a thick patch of gorse. They hid until there was the almost silence of sea-moor – distant surf, wind, the rasp of a stonechat's call, somewhere close a grasshopper chirping.

Bleeding and sore-footed, they stumbled through gorse saplings and heather, pale with shock and fear. Hazel held the hands of

Sand and Lo; Sweetpea, who had scraped her knee and was crying louder than the others, now rode on Sid's shoulders. Between them they carried what they had managed to rescue of Freedom Farm.

As they reached the hamlet above the beach Izzi came racing to him, wagging his tail furiously and barking in greeting.

'Does he bite? asked Hazel, gathering Sand and Lo to her.

'He won't hurt you.' And the children wrapped their small arms around the dog's woolly neck and smiled through their tears, except Sweetpea, who was wary of the bouncy dog and remained on Sid's shoulders.

'He's all wet,' said Sand, rubbing her hands on her shorts.

'He's a water dog,' said Sid. 'You'll see.'

They had been seen by two of the hamlet's inhabitants, who had first heard the dog barking and then children's voices. It was a sound they hadn't heard for a long time. They stood together, holding hands, staring into the distance, holding back tears. Other cottage people tweaked their curtains.

The bedraggled, exhausted, band of refugees came at last to the little cove and saw smoke from the cooking fire. Gulls hung over the sullen sea, yelling at each other.

'Is it the seaside?' Sweetpea, a curly-haired four-year-old with a constantly runny nose turned her watery eyes to Hazel.

'It is, Sweetpea, it is.'

'Can we build a sandcastle?'

Hazel glanced around her anxiously.

Sid tried to reassure them. 'No razor-wire here, is there, eh? No coastguards. Don't worry, it's safe here, really.' He swung the child down onto the path.

The little girls looked wide-eyed at Hazel for her to give the final permission.

'You can, yes, go on.' And the three little ones ran down to the beach and began finding pebbles and shells and building a castle with their hands, as if nothing awful had happened. As if they had not seen the bullet-torn bodies of loved ones. As if it was normal to have been nearly burnt to death under the floor of a caravan. As if they had not been hidden away in a dense wood for as long as they could remember and had not seen the open sky.

'What happened, boy?' Gaz was anxious.

'The rest of the New-Earthers are all dead. These are the only survivors.'

'Reducers?'

Sid nodded.

'Rose?'

Sid nodded again, lowering his eyes.

Gaz looked stricken, and put both hands to his head. He walked down the beach on his own, ignoring the girls. Izzi didn't know who to be with, Gaz or Sid. He ran from one to the other, barking and whining.

Hazel sat on a rock, keening at the sea, her clothes dark with her mother's blood. Sid was suddenly shy with her. He stood close by, but didn't interrupt her in her grief.

Was it really safe for the children to play on the beach? His eyes razed the sky – no helicopters. And Gaz had said that no coastguards bothered with this part of the coast. He'd never seen any. No Runners would attempt to sail here, it was too hazardous a coastline. You had to be a local to know the fierce currents and where rocks and wrecks hid beneath the waves. And it was true: there was no land between here and America apart from the Isles of Scilly – or the one that still existed, if it really did.

Gaz came back along the beach after a while, his face set in a fixed smile. 'Come on, you must be hungry.'

He poked at the fish stew with a stick, adding a handful of mussels and the stalks of snowbell to it. He said to Sid, 'Make up beds for them in the new part, you share with me.'

Hazel washed the children in the buckets of rainwater and dressed them in the change of underwear she had managed to salvage.

'What shall I do with their soiled clothes?' she asked Sid.

'Give them to me. I'll sort them later.'

She untied the bundle of blankets and helped Sid make room in the tiny hut.

'I built this bit,' he said, wanting to impress her.

'Did you?'

'Yeah. Don't worry about Gaz. He's orright, taught me all sorts. Dowsing and that. He's got a sailing boat.'

'A boat?'

'Yeah, we're going to find the safe island – Scilly.'

'Scilly?'

'Haven't you heard about it? Runners' safe island?'

'Thought it was a myth.'

Sid didn't know what a myth was, but didn't want to show his ignorance. 'It's off Land's End.'

She smiled at him and took his hand. 'Thank you for saving us, Sid.'

He felt himself blushing.

'Any time,' he said, his hand burning. It hadn't occurred to him before that moment, that they *could* really sail to Scilly, but he had wanted to give her hope. And thinking about it later, when he was lying awake listening to the sobs of the bereft children, he decided that he would try to persuade Gaz that it would be a good idea, a solution. They would be safe from the Reducers and the TA. There would be other Runners there. They would build a new life together.

CHAPTER TWENTY-SIX

NEXT DAY GAZ got up earlier than usual, long before dawn, when the only sound was the sea's constant roll and boom, the south-westerly wind moaning and sobbing, and distant gulls calling in the dark mist. He took a spade and set off over the fields. The low-hanging sea-fret masked and soaked everything. Diamonds hung heavily from cobwebs. A vixen slunk away from the man smell and the scent of dog that seemed to be part of the man smell.

Sid, when he had drunk some water and washed himself, mended the roof, which still leaked on one side, and washed the children's soiled clothes in rain water. He built a cooking fire. He loved to build a fire. It felt good, right, natural. He felt like a man.

After hanging up the washing on a makeshift washing line, Hazel fed the little ones with the remains of a bread pudding that she had brought from the camp, and spent most of the day searching the rocks for winkles, limpets and mussels, trying not to think of the horrors of the last day in Freedom Farm. She grieved for Moth, her mother. She missed the comfort of the community of women, the communal cooking and sewing. They had shared the care of the children. Now, it seemed that it was all up to her. It was obvious to her that Gaz wanted nothing to do with them, and Sid had other duties around the place. Work was therapeutic. It was when she stopped that the sorrow overwhelmed her.

She had thought that the little ones were remarkably stoic. But today, they were all tearful. Sweetpea in particular, who had always been a difficult child to please. She didn't like fish or shellfish. She didn't like rabbit. She didn't like nuts, she hated green stuff. She had never been sociable and now she refused to have anything to do with the others and she refused to eat. Hazel was anxious about her and when Sid sat down at last she told him.

'Has she tried mushrooms?'

'Yes. Doesn't like them.'

'Apples?'

'Fruit is about the only thing she will eat.'

'If she's hungry enough she'll eat,' said Sid. He was sure his mother had used the same words about Lo when she was being finicky.

It started to rain, drizzle at first, then more heavily. Hazel called the little ones and took them into the shack. They huddled together under the blankets.

'Why did we leave Freedom Farm?' asked Sand. 'I like it there, it's much better. I want donkey.'

Hazel cuddled the child, unable to answer.

'Hello, can I come in?' Sid peered into the muggy room. It was a sad sight. The motherless girl and children, huddled together, all weeping.

'What's this?' he knelt and plucked a seashell from Sweetpea's ear. The little ones looked astonished.

'I want one, I want one,' demanded Sand.

He conjured a cockleshell from her ear, too. Then a small white pebble from Lo's ear.

'It's magic. Sid can do lots of magic,' she said, proudly. The small girls smiled through their tears. Hazel thanked him silently; her black eyelashes heavy with tears. She blinked and smiled at him.

'Do it again, do it again,' they begged.

From Hazel's ear he took a piece of smooth blue beach glass. 'Same colour as your eyes,' he said to her.

Gaz returned late, grey with exhaustion, and instead of going to the shack, he went to a high flat rock way out at the edge of the cove, and sat on his own watching the watery sun drop heavily into the ocean.

Sid was hungry. He scrambled over the rocks to where the man sat hunched. 'Shall I cook tea?' Sid asked.

'Do what you like, boy.' Gaz's voice was quiet and flat with controlled emotion.

Sid was angry. He couldn't manage to look after them all on his own. He cobbled together a meal of boiled rice with a few herbs in, and a dozen mussels opened over the fire. And a pot of herb tea. There weren't enough tin mugs for them all, or dishes, or spoons, and they had to share. Gaz still sat on in the dark, but now Izzi kept him company.

'Is he all right about us being here?' Hazel asked, as she washed the few dishes.

'Course he is. Just unhappy, that's all.'

'Well, so am I!' Hazel sobbed, throwing down the rag she had been using. 'My mother's dead, and all my friends.'

Sid didn't know what to say or do. His throat was tight with grief for his own parents, too, but he couldn't talk about it. At least he had Lo.

Hazel was reading a bedtime story to the children, who were cocooned in blankets and huddled close to her.

'I want to talk to you about something,' Sid said to Gaz, who had been away all day again and now ate on his own outside the shack, away from the sound of children.

He was silent for a while after listening to Sid's plan.

'What makes you think I want to go to Scilly?'

'A helicopter only has to spot one of the kids on the beach and we're all done for. Someone could tell on us. The farmers, perhaps.'

'Your problem, not mine. I didn't ask you to bring them all here. I was all right on my own before you came.'

Gaz threw down his tin plate and walked away to the other end of the beach. Sid spat on the sand and followed him.

Later, Sid and Hazel sat by the dying fire.

'He doesn't want us here, does he?' She held her knees.

'He's a loner, that's all. Not used to lots of kids.'

'What about the island?'

'He's not sure. The boat's only small. It might not get there.' Actually, Gaz had refused outright to consider it. It was too dangerous, they hadn't got a chance of reaching the island. Too many of them for the small boat. But Sid wasn't about to dash her hopes, just like that.

'I see.' Hazel shrugged her shoulders. 'We'll leave. Go find somewhere else to stay.' She straightened her back and stared into the fire.

'No, no, you can't go. Please don't go. I'll look after you.'

She shook her head. 'What about the people up on the hill in the cottages? Might they be able to hide us?' She had no faith in the boy.

'Don't you like it here?'

'The man doesn't want us.'

She lowered her head.

Shy, but determined to comfort her, Sid moved closer and put an arm around her. She leant her head on his shoulder and sobbed.

Gaz kept himself to himself. He reluctantly cooked for them but avoided the youngsters as much as possible, given the cramped living quarters. He went to other coves; he went fishing alone. He festered, not bothering to wash or change his clothes, not talking to Sid. He threw stones at tin cans on rocks. He became morose and uncommunicative. Sid was confused. Gaz had said he could bring Lo back to his hut. Why not the others? It wasn't fair of him.

Even Izzi was affected by his moodiness. He lay next to Gaz, sighing loudly, his head on his paws, his eyes looking sadly from Sid to the man and back to Sid.

After the initial shock and numbness, Sweetpea couldn't shift from her small head the horrors of the day the camp was invaded. She screamed at night as nightmares overtook her. Hazel slept with her, cuddled her and tried to soothe her, but the little girl was inconsolable. Sand was subdued but didn't cry. Hazel was worried about her. Sand seemed content to play during the day, but at night she cried quietly, privately, keeping up a low wail, not able to conjure the comfort of sleep. Dark circles appeared under her eyes, she lost weight. She wet the bed. Hazel had to wash blankets almost every day and dry them on the rocks or the washing line behind the hut.

Izzi was sensitive to the children's grief. He began to howl at night. Gaz tied him to the boat in the cave to muffle the racket.

Sid spent at least an hour each day in the water, swimming. Since his near drowning in the flood he had determined that he would never feel that helpless in water again. He was impervious to the cold, and loved the feeling of power in his arms and shoulders as he crawled through the waves.

'Teach me, Sid, teach me to swim.'

'Okay, Lo, it's easy. See how Izzy does it.' The dog performed with his doggy paddle, barking in joy as the children splashed around him.

Lo learned fast, they all did, running into the surf and letting the waves carry them back to the beach on their tummies. He watched over the girls as if he was a sheep dog watching his flock.

Looking through the stuff in the cave that Gaz had found over the years, Sid found an old surfboard. It was scratched and dented but he sanded it down and waxed it with a stub of candle and spent hours teaching himself to surf on the big rollers that came into the cove. He would lie belly down and paddle out over the surf until the beach was about two hundred yards away. Izzi often swam out to join him, barking happily and wagging his tail behind him. Sid would lie there, waiting for the rise of a good wave, and as he felt the surge take the board under him, he stood, leaning and balancing while the wave sped him past the black rocks into the shallows.

On shore he spent time with Hazel, showing her edible seaweeds and fungi, teaching her the things that he had learned. She, in turn, taught him to cook and sew. Together, they mended the little girls' clothes and patched Gaz's fisherman's smocks. Sid kept pricking his fingers, but he persevered, and she praised the tidiness of his small stitches.

The children went barefoot. One day, Sand trod on a weaver fish in the shallows. She howled with the excruciating pain of the sting from its barb. Sid carried her quickly to the hut and Gaz roused himself to heat a pan of water and hold her foot in it until the pain had eased. He was surprisingly gentle with the small girl, Sid noticed, soothing her cries, wiping her nose for her, and he actually sang a silly song to her until she stopped crying and began to smile. Sid had never heard Gaz sing before.

'Half a pound of tuppeny rice,
Half a pound of treacle,
That's the way the money goes,
Pop goes the weasel.'

At the word *'pop'* he touched the end of her button nose and made her laugh.

'Are you our daddy? asked Sweetpea. The man flushed. He laughed, confused.

'He's my daddy,' said Sand.

'He's my daddy, too,' pronounced Lo.

All of them sat round Gaz, each one trying to control their emotions, though none of them could have said why they felt like crying.

The little girls spent their time playing with Izzi, throwing bits of driftwood into the water for him to retrieve, except Sweetpea, who didn't like dogs. They built fairy castles in the sand, decorating them with shells and pebbles. They splashed in the shallows, showered under the little waterfalls that spurted from the cliff. It took them no time at all to discover the cave and make a den in the boat.

'I'm going to sail the boat,' announced Lo to Sand and Sweetpea.

'Me don't like boats,' said Sweetpea.

'Me don't like boats,' said Sand.

'You're a pooey-face,' shouted Lo, turning her back on them.

'You're a pooey-face, too,' shouted Sand and threw a handful of small pebbles at the departing child.

Hazel decided that it was time the children went back to school. She sat them down on a rock, and read to them. There was no paper for them to write or draw on.

'They could use the charcoal,' she said to Gaz. 'Use the back of your paintings?'

'Do what you like,' he said, walking away. There's been no drawing or painting for him since the girls had arrived. There was no peace, no room, no way to escape first the sounds of grief, then later, the squeals and shrieks of small children playing. More than anything, he was missing Rose.

One bright windy day, Sid said, 'What date is it?'

'Ninth April,' said Gaz, 'or thereabouts.' He had a calendar of sorts, which he had drawn on one wall of their room.

'I think it's my birthday.' Sid beamed.

'Seriously? How old are you?' said Hazel.

'Sixteen,' he lied.

'We'll have a party.'

Hazel organised the three little ones to build a birthday cake with sand and pebbles, little twigs as candles. That evening, after another supper of limpets and mussels, and with a rare tin of beans, she got them all to sit in a circle around the sandcastle, even Gaz. Each girl had found or made him a present – Sand found a perfectly round white pebble; Hazel made a belt of shells with holes in strung onto a length of blue nylon that she had found on the beach, and Sweetpea found a mermaid's purse – a white cluster of whelk egg sacks. Lo presented him with a perfect sea urchin skeleton. 'It looks like a potato, doesn't it?' she said, and gave him a big kiss. They sang Happy Birthday, except Gaz, who sat morosely silent.

The cooking fire was dying, and Hazel took Sid's hand as they sat and gazed into the embers.

'I need to go back to Freedom,' she said. 'There might be things we could use.'

'I think the fire destroyed it all.'

'There's bound to be stuff that's survived.'

'I'll come with you.'

'I don't want to leave the children with Gaz. He won't look after them.'

'I'll ask him to,' said Sid.

'I don't trust him. He doesn't like us.'

'He's unhappy, is all. He loved Rose, I think.' Sid was

embarrassed to use the word 'love'.

'He's not kind to us.'

'Give him time.'

They sat quietly, leaning together, shoulder touching shoulder, hip touching hip. Sid felt the warmth of her body close to his. Her warm hand in his. It was the best birthday he had ever had.

'Where were you before Freedom?' he asked her.

'With Mum, in St Ives. She was a school-teacher.'

'St Ives? I was near there: Hayle. Lo and me were hiding on a roundabout.'

'Roundabout? Wasn't it rather exposed? Hayle is where the Reducer Headquarters is.'

'Nah, covered in bushes and trees, it was. Well hidden. It was okay there. I got water from a lake. Met a Reducer. Saved his life.'

'Saved his life?'

He didn't need much persuasion to relate the story.

Hazel regarded the boy at her side. Although she was older than Sid, she realised that he was the more experienced. He was strong and clever with his hands. He was gentle with his little sister and the other children. He had survived adventures she could only imagine.

'How come you ended up in Freedom?' he asked.

'We were too near the Reducer base. Mum was scared we would be taken.'

'What about your dad?'

'He left years ago. Don't know where he is now. Never kept in touch, except sometimes for my birthday.' She sounded bitter, and he felt ashamed for the man.

'How did you know about Freedom Farm?'

'Mum had a friend who knew about it and we made a run for it, or rather, a walk and scramble! Took the coast path. Other women eventually arrived; we all helped build the camp.'

'Why did they take Lo?' It had been worrying him, that the women were supposed to be good but had kidnapped his sister. Hazel stood and began to walk along the beach, the wind tugging at the chain of sea pinks in her hair. Sid scrambled up and joined her.

'She was alone in an old train carriage, wasn't she? They saved her.'

'But I was only gone for an hour.'

'They weren't to know that, were they? Storm said there was a disgusting old man hanging about. Anything could have happened to her. Storm was always looking for lost girls.'

'Why only girls?'

'She has – had – a theory – men were the root of all evil in the world – wars, weapons, technology, the Warming, The Emergency.'

'But…' Sid felt guilty without knowing why. Guilt about leaving Lo on her own; guilt by association. He couldn't help being a boy, could he? It wasn't his fault. Somehow the day was spoiled.

Oystercatchers piped as they flew across the darkening beach. Small waves fell and sucked at the pebbles, rolling them back and forth. Crows pecked at seaweed on the edge of the sea. A peregrine hovered above the cliff. Bats flitted across the beach.

Next day, Gaz went with Sid to Freedom, leaving Hazel in charge.

'You best not go back there, my flower.' Gaz told her. 'You stay here and look after the little'uns.'

It was a relief for her not to go. She saw in her mind the dead bodies, smelt the burning flesh again, and shuddered. Hazel gave them a list of things to look for at the camp and where to find them. A sea-fret hung over the beach and the children wanted to stay indoors and play, but she shooed them outside. 'A little rain won't hurt you.' While they were out of the way she tidied the hut, shaking the blankets of sand and washing their few clothes, humming to herself and clicking her tongue at the untidiness of men. She hung the dripping clothes on the washing line in the fine drizzle, and propped up the sagging line with a long pole with a notch in the top that Sid had whittled specially. She picked a bunch of late heather from the cliff behind the shack and squeezed them into a jar. Hopefully, Sid would bring back extra mugs and dishes from Freedom Farm. Freedom – she couldn't bear to think about the terrible scenes they had fled from. Grief struck her suddenly and she sank to the floor and held her head in her hands. It was like that. She could go for a day or two without thinking about her mother and friends, and then, for no apparent reason, the loss came roaring back.

Sand and Pink made pebble patterns on the beach, but Sweetpea, cross about being made to go out in the rain, and unusually bold, ran off to be by herself on the far side of the cove, where she found a narrow path going up and away from the others. She plucked at daisies growing next to the path, and picked two small red berries and ate them. They didn't taste very good but she pretended they were sweeties and ate another before spitting it out. She crouched and watched insects – a grasshopper rubbed its back legs together. A spider hid in the corner of a torn, sparkling web. She blew bubbles of spit and spat at a blue hoverfly. A young rabbit hopped nearby, nibbling at the sweet damp grass. It disappeared over the edge and she followed it. Leaning over to see where it had gone she slipped on the wet grass and fell.

CHAPTER TWENTY-SEVEN

THEY CAME TO THE VALLEY of nut trees, filled a bag with hazelnuts and left it by a hedge to pick up on their return. The stink of smoke and death still hung like a grey veil or an autumn sea-fret. Sid hung back, nervous about going back to Freedom. Izzi ran ahead, curious, his muzzle lifted to sniff the smell of old smoke and other interesting scents.

'Where are all the bodies?' Sid stared around him.

'Buried them.'

'On your own?'

'Who else was going to do it?'

'I'd have helped if you'd asked.'

'Yeah, well, not a job for a kid.'

'I'm not a kid,' Sid said angrily.

'Keep your hair on, boy.' Gaz grinned for the first time since he had lost Rose. Sid did have more hair these days; it was almost down to his shoulders.

Searching through the burnt-out vans they took what was left – a roll of linen and sewing cottons; a bag of rice, only slightly chewed by mice; a rolling pin, needles, scissors, a good carving knife, a block of salt and a flask of elderflower wine. Pots and pans, tin plates and mugs went into the sacks. They were getting heavy. Gaz swooped jubilantly on a large paintbrush, and Sid found a couple of tomato plants in pots that hadn't been lost in the blaze.

A line of washing hung limp and blackened by smoke. Sid

unpegged shorts, T-shirts, and underwear. They'd be all right after a couple of washes, he thought, and Hazel would be delighted to have more clothes.

To their amazement a chicken still stalked the woods, all alone, clucking to herself.

'Didn't see her before,' said Gaz.

She ran to them, expecting food, and they caught her easily, tied her legs together and carried her with them, upside down. She didn't seem to mind. She had laid several eggs but they weren't sure how old they were, so they left them for rat and badger. She would lay more.

Sid came across the graveyard under the lime tree. Each mound of earth had a rock or a log at its head and the name of the dead marked in pebbles. A few limp nasturtiums lay on Rose's grave. Sid realised that Gaz must have known these women well. The smaller mounds were of Hazel's friends, the girls he had seen laughing with her.

He whistled for the dog. They staggered back over the moors with their burden of provisions, and stopped in the middle of the high moor to rest.

A cold easterly wind blew. A thin-faced vixen ran across the blustery field. Izzi watched the fox but made no attempt to chase after it.

A kestrel hung, quivering.

They arrived back at the cove, their arms aching from the heavy sacks and were met by a tearful Hazel.

'I can't find Sweetpea,' she sobbed. 'I've searched everywhere.'

'Where was she when you last saw her?' Gaz was furious. *Bleddy kids, nothing but trouble!*

'I don't know. She was with the others.' Her eyes were red from crying.

'Where did she go, Lo-lo?' Sid asked the unconcerned child.

'Over there?' She pointed vaguely in the wrong direction. 'Anyway, she's a pooey-face,' and she went back to making pretend biscuits from limpet shells, while Sand tried to leap over a big sandcastle

'Stay and watch them,' Sid said to Hazel. She nodded, anxious to do the right thing.

They searched unsuccessfully for a while then Gaz gave Izzi one of the children's blankets to sniff. The dog set off at a trot across the beach, followed closely by Sid and Gaz. Izzi wagged his tail and sniffed at the sand and pebbles. He nosed up the path that Sweetpea had taken and stood at the top barking wildly and wagging his tail. Gaz and Sid leaned over to look. The child lay on a ledge about twenty feet down, like a crumpled and broken doll.

'Get a rope,' ordered Gaz. 'Don't let them come up here.'

Sid ran back to the hut and took a coil of rope from a hook. He avoided Hazel's eyes.

'Have you found her? Is she hurt?'

'She fell. Stay here.' Hazel wrung her hands and sobbed. Lo and Sand were digging in the sand and making puddles of water in which they floated mussel shell boats.

They buried her above the beach of the next cove. It was a sorrowful group who sat around the fire that evening. Hazel was heartbroken, her face swollen and red.

'It was my fault. I should have watched them better. I should have watched them.' Sid didn't know what to say to her.

After the death of Sweetpea, the others were subdued. Gaz kept himself to himself, getting on with chores without asking for Sid's help. Sid didn't know how to comfort Hazel. She was inconsolable.

'I'll never forgive myself, never. I should have kept her safe. I never should have let them play by themselves.'

Sand was quiet and tearful, sleeping more than normal, but had formed an attachment to the hen, which she followed around, clucking to it.

Lo was the only one who didn't seem affected by the death. She made elaborate sandcastles and decorated them with shells and weed. She played at dens in the boat in the cave, pretending that the Angel was there and she was looking after him. She spent hours prodding at the waving fronds of dark red anemones in little rock pools, hoping they would tug at her finger, and watching hermit shells walk. One day she found a pale blue starfish with a missing arm. Gaz told her it would grow another one, but she didn't believe him.

'If I lost an arm, would I grow another one?'

'No, you wouldn't.'

'Why wouldn't I?'

'Because you wouldn't.'

'Will you grow another finger?'

'No, I won't.'

'But if a starfish can do it, why can't you?'

'Oh my giddy aunt!' Gaz stomped off with his fishing rod.

Helicopters were searching the moors behind them. They could hear the throb of the rotors. Izzi twitched his expressive ears at the hated noise. Sid took to keeping watch on the bluff above the beach, hiding in the thick bushes that grew by the stream. He noted the number of sorties the helicopters made and kept track of their journeys. It seemed to him that they were getting closer each day. Were they searching for Runners?

One day, he smelt the warm scent of bread coming from the farm cottage. He lifted his head like a dog sniffing out a rabbit. Izzi woofed.

The woman stood in her small front garden again, sprigs of rosemary in her hands.

'Hello there,' she called. 'You all right, then?'

Sid was torn between his natural tendency to be polite and his loyalty to Gaz, who, he knew, didn't talk to her. He nodded and looked away, embarrassed. She went back to searching the sky, listening to the helicopter. He didn't feel safe at the beach any more. He found Gaz fishing from a rock.

'I think we should move. We're putting you at risk by being here. I'll take the others somewhere else, move back to the roundabout.'

'Right, lad, we've got to make plans.'

'Plans?'

'You still want to go to the island?'

'Scilly? Yes!'

'Right then. I'll take you.'

'Really? Would you really? Oh thank you, Gaz.' He hugged the man fiercely, but Gaz shoved him off.

'I'll need to ready the boat.'

'I'll help. I'll do anything you want.'

'Yeah, you're a good lad.' Gaz sniffed and spat.

Sid was over the moon. This was the answer, sail to the island. See if they could survive there. Wanting to please Gaz, he asked, 'Caught anything?' He looked into the keep-net that dragged in the water.

'Couple of big garfish.' The man was pleased with the catch.

Sid said, 'I like garfish.'

The eel-like fish with bright green bones was grilled that night on sticks over the fire. They sat round the embers in a small circle, and Sid told Hazel what had been decided.

Later, he couldn't sleep for excitement and anxiety at the idea of setting off once again on yet another journey. Running.

CHAPTER TWENTY-EIGHT

THEY TURNED THE BOAT upside down and scraped the barnacles off its bottom. Sid and Hazel patched small tears in the sail. Sid sanded off the flaking paint and retouched the hull with a small tin of varnish that Gaz had stored in the cave. Gas repainted the name, *Girl Rose,* slowly and carefully with red paint, admired his own handiwork, wiped his bleary eyes and coughed up phlegm.

He renewed some of the ropes, splicing new shanks onto the frayed bits. He retrieved some old plastic cans with stoppers from the cave, where he'd stored them for a rainy day, tied them together and shoved them before the mast for extra buoyancy. He scrubbed the rudder and centre plate.

'She be ship-shape now,' he said, regarding his craft. He had two proper lifebelts already, and he cobbled together three flotation belts from corks and plastic floats held together with cord. He stowed these beneath the thwarts. He checked that the hand pump was oiled and secured it under the fore-hatch with cord.

A sad-eyed man crouched on the bluff watching Gaz coming and going, busy with repairs to the boat. He had seen the children playing on the beach before this. He observed closely the preparations that were being made. He knew Gaz of old, had had dealings with him before, but he hadn't spoken to him for years, not since they had fought over his wife. He'd heard that Gaz had had another woman since, a few miles away, but he and she had split up. He thought there had been a child, but he didn't listen to gossip. Knowing Gaz, there was probably more than one. And when the Reduction began Gaz had left the hamlet to live on the beach. Since that time they had had no contact with him.

Washing the dishes after their supper, the farmer told his wife what he had seen. She knew about the children on the beach, of course. They all knew what was going on. News, especially bad news, travelled fast in the countryside. The people at the hamlet had heard of the destruction of the women's camp. They were aware that Gascoigne was harbouring Runners. But they had lived in fear since The Emergency. They didn't want to draw attention to themselves. So far, the TA and Reducers had left them alone since the year before, when all illegals had been taken away.

Grief was still raw for both of them. They cried together again over a photograph of their lost daughter and grand-daughter, who they had loved more than life itself. The woman sat on a lower bunk bed and rearranged the soft toys on the pillow, dreaming and crying softly. Next day they went back to the bluff and watched the children playing.

Gaz spotted them but made no sign.

He planned to sail on an outgoing tide at dusk, on a day when the wind blew in a favourable direction. It was a long way in a small boat, heavily loaded, sailing through dangerous waters, where larger vessels had come to grief over the years. He showed the boy the tattered map he still had. It was a chart of the waters between Land's End and the islands. They weren't sailing from Land's End, but he felt pretty confident that he could find his way there in the dark from the cove.

'They look very small.' Sid was surprised at the small dots that were the islands. 'How do we know which one still exists?' He was beginning to wonder whether it had been such a good idea.

'I'll get you there, don't you fret,' said the man, carefully folding the taped-together, fragile chart that he had managed to stick onto another piece of paper to strengthen it.

The day before the voyage the farmer and his wife visited the cove. Izzi woofed quietly.

'Someone's coming, Gaz.'

'What do *they* want?' the man said, bad-temperedly.

'Good morning Gascoigne.'

Gaz grunted.

'Wouldn't bother you, only we have a plan,' said the farmer, dropping the sack full of provisions they had brought – cake, honey, beets, potatoes, biscuits and dried beans. He had an angular brown face, weathered by sea winds, lined with sorrow. His eyebrows were bushy and grey, though his hair was still youthfully black and his eyes were clear blue. 'Here's our idea. We'll take the little girls and look after them as if they were our own.'

Gaz, Sid, Hazel and the little girls stood silent. It was an unexpected development.

'But don't you want to come in the boat to the island with us?' Hazel asked Lo and Sand.

'Me don't like boats,' said Sand.

'I want to go with Sid and Hazel,' said Lo, grabbing Sid's hand as if he was about to leave her there and then.

'Wasn't there another one?' asked the woman.

'Fell off the cliff,' said Gaz, quietly.

Hazel started to sob.

'Oh, my dear Lord, come here, my flower.' The woman held her and tried to comfort her.

'Can you keep Sand safe?' Hazel asked, sniffing back the tears.

'Yes, we can. As if she was one of our own.' She was a good-looking woman with white wiry hair, a determined mouth and gentle brown eyes.

'What do you think, Sand? Would you like to stay with …? I'm sorry, I don't know your name.'

'Stella, she's called Stella. She'll take care of her,' said Gaz, not looking directly at the woman.

'We've got a cat that just had three kittens.' The farmer, whose name was James Craze, crouched down so that he was at Sand's level and smiled at her.

That did it. The child nodded shyly and took his hand. Lo was tempted by the idea of a kitten, but she had Izzi, so she didn't mind. And anyway, she wouldn't dream of leaving Hazel and Sid.

'What about you, then, my maid?' The farmer looked at Hazel. 'You can come and live along of us if you like.'

'No, thank you, I want to go with Sid.' She went to him and took his hand.

Sid's heart soared. He grinned from ear to ear.

After half an hour of further preparations for the voyage, the Crazes helped Gaz and Sid push the loaded boat into the water.

'Safe journey.'

Sand stood between them on the beach, holding the clucking hen, and waved. Izzi barked back at them from the stern of *Girl Rose*.

'Be good, be safe,' called Lo to Sand.

Hazel had an emotional parting with Sand, but the small child was callous as only young children know how to be. She had been promised a proper bedroom with bunk beds, pictures on the walls, pink curtains, kittens and toys. What more could she possibly want? And she had no idea of time and distance, no idea that maybe she would never see Hazel again, but Hazel knew and was sad. Above them on the bluff, the rest of the hamlet's survivors were watching and wishing them God-speed.

Gaz sailed towards the setting sun, taking their bearings along the coastline, keeping the boat close to the cliffs, but far enough out so that they weren't drawn onto the rocks. The sea was quiet. The wind was not too fierce, but strong enough to speed them along in the gathering gloom. They passed a group of ancient engine houses on the cliff edge, tall ruined towers, like broken teeth.

'They're tin mines,' Sid told Hazel, 'aren't they, Gaz?'

Gaz grunted. He had a lot to think about. His ancient chart showed the main rocks, wrecks and hazards. But he wasn't sure of his ability to sail his boat all the way to the island, any more. He wasn't as strong as he used to be, or as confident. But he knew his night sky and could steer by the stars.

Gulls flew with them, quiet for once. They came to Land's End, the old buildings abandoned to crows and bats. The harsh cry of a chough followed them out to sea.

As they left the shadow of the ragged cliffs, Sid felt as if he was leaving everything he had ever known. He had come a long way from home, driven out by The Emergency: a refugee, a Runner, responsible for the safety of his little sister. He thought of his mother's pleading eyes, his silent promise to look after Lo. And he had, more or less, apart from the time she was taken by the New-Earthers. But he had her again, and she was safe. His mam would be proud of him. And his dad. He had learned many things – to fire a rifle, make a cooking fire, use a lance, grow food, sail a boat, so many other skills. Sid was looking forward to whatever might happen on the island he thought of in his head as Runners' Island.

'See the lighthouse? Longships, it's called.' There was no light, there had been no light for years, but a tall dark shape loomed ahead. 'We have to go that way, past it.' Gaz steered and Sid had control of the sail. Izzi had settled down at Hazel's feet and Lo was asleep in Hazel's arms.

'How long will it take?' asked Hazel.

'Dunno. Fourteen, fifteen hours at this rate, if we're lucky, wind stays aft of us.' Gaz concentrated on the sky and the straining sail. A sliver of moon smiled on them.

'Why are we sailing in the dark?' asked Hazel.

'Safer this way. Don't want any coastguards to see us,' said Gaz.

'Thought you said there weren't any coastguards?'

'Best be safe than sorry.'

'Look!' Sid pointed. At least a dozen dolphins dived and curved at the prow of the boat, keeping pace with them.

Lo, wakened by Hazel, hung over the side, laughing every time the dolphins leaped out of the water. Phosphorescence gleamed and fanned behind them.

'Thought they were extinct,' said Hazel, thrilled.

'Maybe they're Runners, like us,' said Sid.

They dozed and woke, dozed and woke, too uncomfortable to rest properly. Sid took the helm for a while so that Gaz could have a sleep, but the man didn't trust the boy to handle the laden boat on his own, and kept up a torrent of orders: 'Too close to the wind, boy, ease her off a bit.' And 'Going off course, ain't you boy? Tack now, I say.' He had no rest to speak of but insisted on taking over the helm.

Hazel and Lo slept little; they were cold and wet from the spray that came over the sides and bow. Hazel sang to the little girl but nothing helped. Lo was violently sick in the boat.

Gaz scooped a bail of water from the sea and threw it onto the vomit in the bilges. It swam the length of the little boat and back again. Sid and Hazel lifted their feet.

Hazel held the little girl's hair away from her face as she was sick again, this time over the side of the boat, away from the wind.

'Watch the horizon, Lo,' Sid told her, 'then you won't feel ill.' Gaz had told him that the first time they had gone fishing in bad weather.

'What's the 'rizon?' she whispered.

'Where the sea meets the sky.' But there was no horizon, only the towering blackness of rolling waves. A terrifying wall of water bearing down on them, receding as they rose and breached the wave, then rising up again and again, seemingly to engulf them. They gave up trying to avoid the vomit that swam around in the bottom of the boat and the cold spray that flew at them and drenched them. The waves were longer now, and taller. Every time the boat fell down into the deep trough of a wave Hazel thought that they would never come out of it. It was lucky that it was dark, she thought, she didn't want to see the size of the waves and the vast expanse of ocean.

'It's a long time to be in a little boat, for a child,' she accused no one in particular. What choice had they, really? she thought. Where else could they go to be safe? She had put her trust in Sid and Gaz, and now she had to live with it. Put up with the terror of being in a small boat in a big sea, with only hope to get them to safety. She had lost her mother at the camp, lost her friends, lost Sweetpea, and left Sand behind, and now there was only Sid and Lo.

'Bad luck, women in a boat,' Gaz grumbled to himself. 'Daft idea, this. Should never have agreed to it.'

It was indeed a foolhardy journey to make, especially in the dark and with no compass. What had he been thinking of? He wasn't a young man any longer, and his cough troubled him, and made his lungs sore.

Rose, his woman, came into his mind. She had adored him, for a while, until their boy died. He felt the usual bitterness when he remembered the death of his only son, Matthew. It had hit the boy so quickly, the terrible flu that had killed in a couple of days. The worst flu epidemic to hit the world since the 1940s, they said. It was God's way of keeping down the numbers, some said. Their little girl had been born at Freedom Farm. And now he had let his old adversary, James Craze, have the child. But Stella was a good woman, strong, resourceful. The child would have a good life with them.

Lo was wishing that she and Sid were in that other boat on the lake near the roundabout. She had liked it there. There were dragonflies and once they had seen a kingfisher diving to catch a small fish. At least, Sid had seen it and told her about it. She wasn't sick in that boat. 'Are we there yet?' she asked the dark.

They had been sailing for over twelve hours in a moderate breeze, when a violent squall hit the boat. It surged forward plunging into the waves. Hazel huddled, soaked, with Lo in the bottom. Izzi stood on the bow like a figurehead, not the least bothered by the motion, wagging his tail. Sid was exhilarated and scared, but Gaz seemed unconcerned. He sat in the stern, both hands on the straining tiller, while Sid controlled the sail, his hands blistered and sore from the wet, tugging rope.

'Tighten your lifebelt straps,' said Gaz, and Hazel reached across to refasten Lo's lifebelt. The child was asleep from exhaustion.

'Are we in any danger, Gaz?' asked Sid.

'Sailing's always dangerous,' Gaz muttered to himself, 'if you don't know what you're doing.' Clouds obscured the moon and stars. It was difficult keeping to the course he had decided on. He had to trust his instincts. A compass would have been good, but he had no such luxury.

'Nah, boy,' he added. 'Not really in danger, as long as we don't hit a rock or get blown off course. In which case we'll end up in America.' He grinned to himself. He liked a challenge. It had been a long time since he had come this far. He thought of the gig race to Scilly that time. He had been young and fit, broad-shouldered and handsome. The crew had had such a good time, even though they hadn't won the race. It was a mixed crew, men and women, Stella being one of them. She was a strong rower and a good laugh. He and she had had fun in those days, before she had met the farmer. He spat away from the wind. It was a good feeling, being in charge, doing something well. He felt the craft answer to his steering. 'I'll have that main sheet now, he said, 'Cleat it.' Sid thankfully fastened the rope that controlled the lugsail and passed the knotted end to the man.

'Aye, aye, Cap'n,' he shouted over the roar of the sea.

Gaz considered putting a reef or two in the sail as the wind was getting lively, but he left it as it was. They'd get there faster if he left the boat in full sail. 'Get some rest, boy,' he said. He raised the centre plate a little.

Sid and Hazel lay, cramped, wet and tired, Lo dozing between them while the boat surged ahead into the dark. They held hands over the child's restless body. She woke once and whimpered, 'Mammy?' gazed unseeing at the dark sea and sky, the fast purple clouds, the odd star, and fell back into their arms. Gaz kept looking up, now and then recognising a star or two to help them on their way. He coughed and spat, coughed and spat. They were running fast before the wind, when the wind suddenly veered and changed direction. With no warning, the boat gybed, swinging the sail fast across the boat, and the heavy boom knocked him on the head.

Sid slept and dreamed that he was working with Brunel, on the half-built bridge over the Tamar. The only way to cross was by basket slung from an iron rail, hundreds of feet up. He was halfway across together with Brunel when the roller stuck and he had to climb over the side of the basket to un-stick the roller.

'Go on boy, you can do it,' said Sid's hero. For some reason he sounded like his dad. He launched himself over and woke to find himself floundering in water. He gasped for breath, not understanding where he was or what was happening. He heard screams, felt the weight of the sail on top of him, pushing him down. He thought he was going to die. He was pressed deeper into the icy cold. Lifting his arms above him he slipped out of the lifebelt and left it tangled in the ropes of the sail. He plunged down away from the submerged sail and came up a short distance from the capsized craft, which was drifting fast away from him. He remembered what Gaz had told him about never leaving a capsized boat to drift away. In two strokes he was beside the upside down boat, grabbing at the bow rope. He hung onto it and swam with one arm towards the vague shapes in the fast water. The weight of the boat pulled at his arm, slowing his progress. He was tempted to let go, but he didn't. If he lost the boat they would all drown.

'Lo?' She was floating on her back, her face pale and still as a moon.

'I'm coming, Lo.' He swam to her and held onto her lifebelt. Hazel was flailing nearby, coughing and spluttering, and Gaz seemed to be unconscious in the water, barely afloat. The dog grabbed the man's flotation belt in his teeth and paddled with him towards Sid.

'Hang onto Lo,' Sid spluttered at Hazel over the roar of the sea.

He took a deep breath and dived under the boat. Unlike the practice capsize he had performed with Gaz, this time the boat had turned turtle. It was upside down. What should he do? The centre-plate! Feeling his way through the heavy sail, he felt for and pushed the centre-plate back into place. The mast had fallen out of its casing. He pulled at it and it swung up to the surface, the heavy sail wallowing. Still under the boat, being tugged by the waves, he lowered the lugsail and wrapped it onto the boom, fastening it. Out of breath, he rose to the surface and made sure everyone was still floating. Frozen to his bones, but determined to live, he manhandled the boat so it was facing into the wind. He clambered onto the upside down hull, stood on the side, and pulled at the centre plate to haul the *Girl Rose* right side up. Waves hid the others from him, but he knew he had to get the boat back in action or they would all die. He slowly dragged it upright, manhandled the mast into its footing, untied and yanked up the lugsail a little way and made the rope fast, set the rudder and tiller, and headed towards the drifting survivors, trying to bail out the water with one hand. He let go the shortened sail to halt the boat, and while the wet canvas flapped wildly, he lifted Lo out of the waves first. The small girl was nearly at the end of her endurance. She had swallowed a lot of seawater, and Sid pumped her chest to help her expel it. Hazel helped him pull and push Gaz over the side into the boat and then had to wait until more water was emptied from the hull before she pulled herself in. They bailed out as fast as they could. Gaz was still unconscious, his head bleeding. Lo sobbed and shivered uncontrollably. The dog paddled furiously next to the boat, trying to get into it.

'Help Izzi,' shouted Sid, fighting to keep the waterlogged boat afloat and upright in the strong gusts. Hazel managed to lift the dog to safety. Izzi shook himself and licked Gaz's bloody face.

'Good dog,' she said. They were all exhausted by their ordeal and suffering from the cold.

'Is he all right?' Sid nodded towards the man.

'I think so.'

'Orright, Lo-lo?'

Her teeth chattered so much she couldn't speak. Her lips were blue.

'Carry on bailing. There's too much water in here,' he told Hazel. 'You too, Lo, do what Hazel's doing.'

'I can't,' she whimpered.

'You must.' He knew her small hands wouldn't be of much use, but at least she'd keep moving and it might help her warm up. But Lo was too tired, too cold.

The wind dropped as quickly as it had developed, and the moon appeared between huge clouds, showing a dark shape on the horizon, before it was obscured again. Sid reefed the sail even more, folding and tying it to the boom. and pulled the shortened canvas up the mast. The half submerged boat dropped sickeningly into the troughs between waves and each time Sid doubted it would rise above the next. He had no idea whether it was the land-mass of Cornwall that he had glimpsed, or the island, but he steered the boat in that direction. It was their only hope.

He hung onto the tiller, feeling the drag of the waterlogged craft. Gaz was still unconscious.

Hazel sobbed, 'Sid, she's not right, she's not right. I can't wake her.' She held Lo in her shivering arms. The little girl was limp, lifeless. She couldn't feel her breathing.

Sid was torn between having to steer the boat, keep it sailing towards what he thought was land, and taking his little sister in his arms. '*Look after my baby.*' His mam's last words to him.

He couldn't do this. They were all going to die.

Izzi barked and staggered about, frantic, licking Gaz's face, clambering over the thwarts to Sid, then going back to the inert man.

Gaz coughed and vomited salt water. Opening his eyes, he took in the situation at once and searched for and found the hand-pump, where he had stored it, tied under the bow thwart. Very soon the boat was floating a bit higher in the water, and he took Lo from Hazel, and rubbed the child's body to try and warm her. Hazel now desperately worked the hand-pump. Sid, searching the blackness of sea and now starless sky for the elusive landmass, held tight to the sluggish tiller. He steered to a vague, blacker, darkness and prayed.

'You're bleeding,' Lo said, her teeth chattering again.

'She's alive,' said Gaz, crying with joy. 'She's alive.'

Izzi barked and leapt past everyone to his usual position in the bow, where he bounced up and down in excitement and taking the bow rope in his jaws, plunged into the water. He swam strongly, dragging the boat along.

'What's he doing?' called Sid from the stern.

'Leading us, he's leading us!' Hazel yelled. 'Look!'

A dark mass. The island! They could see faint dots of light, like fallen stars. No, they were torches. Not wreckers? The thought flickered briefly into Sid's mind. He'd heard about people who had led ships onto rocks to be wrecked and stolen the craft's cargo, long ago. But no, the dim beams were showing them the way to a safe harbour. On their right was a high cliff, or maybe it was a pier. Lights flickered high up. They swung past the dark wall. A slipway appeared then disappeared in the waves that swept over it. People shouted.

'I'll take her in,' said Gaz, handing Lo over to Hazel. He lifted the cork fenders over the side.

'No, I'll do it,' said Sid. He uncleated the mainsheet and the sail slid down the mast. The boat slowed. Sid skilfully steered and eased the drifting boat up to the steep slipway, leapt over the side as a wave lifted them, just as if he was leaping from one roof to another. He landed safely, staggered slightly, but regained his balance and fastened the stern rope to an old metal capstan. Izzi clambered up onto dry land, offered the other rope to Sid and shook himself, barking and wagging his tail vigorously.

CHAPTER TWENTY-NINE

A SMALL GROUP of people waited on the jetty with towels and blankets.

'Heard the dog barking, we did.'

'Runners, eh?'

They gathered round the bedraggled group, who could hardly stand.

'You come along of us,' said a woman. Lo and Hazel were wrapped in blankets and taken next door. Sid and Gaz were whisked off to another cottage, but not before the men had helped secure the boat safely.

After a hot shower – heaven! – and wearing borrowed huge pyjamas and dressing gown, and hugging a mug of hot milk – such bliss! – Hazel gazed around the small room. It felt odd, being in a proper house. The walls were of granite, but it was pretty. Flowery curtains were drawn across the window and coloured rag rugs sang on the wood floor. A solid-fuel stove warmed the small room. A black and white cat slept on an embroidered cushion on one of two armchairs, her ears pricked forward. Salt water still ran from Hazel's nose. She mopped at it with the corner of the towel that wrapped her wet hair like a turban. She smiled but couldn't stop shivering.

Lo didn't stay awake long enough to drink all of her hot milk and honey. The woman had bathed her and rubbed her in a warmed blanket until she was pink again. She hadn't slept in a proper bed for a long time and fell asleep immediately, hugging a hot water bottle with a fluffy teddy bear cover.

Sid and Gaz were given mugs of tea, warm towels and dry clothes. Gaz was given first aid for the injury to his head and a large plaster covered the cut. The happy dog sat at their feet by an open fire, head on paws, gazing lovingly at them. Every now and then either Sid or Gaz would reach out to him and ruffle the fur on his head and speak proudly about him, and Izzi thumped his tail lazily.

But before they were shown where to sleep, Sid insisted on going next door to check on his sister. With Hazel at his side, he stood at the foot of the child's bed and gazed at the peaceful picture – Lo was snuggled up under the heavy blankets, her fluffy pale hair spread on the white pillow. Her little face was pink. She was peacefully asleep. Another little girl was next to her in the same bed.

'That's Doll,' whispered the woman, 'She's my baby.' The female cat jumped up and settled at the children's feet, purring gently. Hazel took Sid's hand and smiled at him. 'You saved us all, Sid, saved our lives. Thank you.' And she reached up to his face and kissed his smooth cheek.

Sid fell asleep almost immediately his head hit the pillow but was woken a couple of hours later by Gaz, snoring. The painter had abandoned his comfortable mattress for the rug on the wooden floor. It was Izzi who now spread his woolly body across the bed next to Sid, on his back, legs in the air. Sid smiled to himself in the dark.

Next morning they woke to wreaths of sea mist covering the island and harbour. Gaz was up first to check on his boat. Remarkably, there was no damage. Izzi accompanied him and walked around in the shallow water lapping on the harbour beach, nuzzling at crabs, pawing the floating weed. Hazel and Sid, after separate breakfasts, took a walk together along the little harbour wall past the cottages, where chickens pecked in an open field, stepping delicately between the feet of goats and a cow.

A wren darted in and out of the top of an evergreen escalonia bush, appearing and disappearing like a diving bird. They passed cultivated fields of potatoes and Brussels sprouts, salad leaves and tomatoes, leafless belladonna lilies dotted between the rows of vegetables. Speckled-breasted thrushes walked and hopped along the rows spearing snails and caterpillars.

The boy and girl reached the top of Telegraph Hill, where a tall tower stood looking over the island. Sid pointed out the date inscribed on the granite – 1805. They climbed the tower and looked down through the blue clear water under which shone a white sand beach that revealed itself as the mist rose and swirled. The sound of hammering came from a yard where three men were building a boat. A small patch of blue appeared in the sky and light sparkled in a patch on the calm water like a thousand silver stars.

'It's perfect, Sid, isn't it?' They sat on a grassy patch and he made a daisy chain for her hair. When they went back towards the cottage they were confronted with what looked like the entire population of the island.

They all gathered in the old pub. Sid noted that the people were clean and well fed, and dressed in clean, patched clothes, with sturdy shoes. The questions poured out.

'What news is there from the mainland?'

'Are there still Reducers?'

'TA still in control of Cornwall, is it?'

'Are there any animals left?'

'There's rabbits,' said Lo, proudly. 'And a milk-cow,' she added, clasping the hand of her new friend, Doll.

'Are you the only people here?' asked Sid of one of the men whose cottage he had slept in.

'Used to be more, but most of the able-bodied have left to find higher lands – Wales or Ireland, Scotland maybe. More of us intend sailing off soon, if you're interested, lad?'

There were half a dozen children and three babies, and an old man and woman. The other islanders were about the same age as his parents, or younger. Several of the women were far gone in pregnancy.

'Well, with you, there are now thirty-five of us, and you're very welcome,' said one of the men they had met the night before. He seemed to be in charge.

'Make that thirty-four,' said Gaz.

'What do you mean, Gaz?' Sid looked at him.

'I'm not staying,' he said. 'Got to get back, thank you kindly.' He tentatively put a finger to his injured forehead.

'But you said…'

'I said I'd bring you, not stay, boy.'

'But we need you, Gaz,' he implored.

'You don't need me, not no more, you don't.' The stern-faced, weather-beaten man put a hand on Sid's shoulder and smiled gently at him. Sid was surprised to realise that they were practically the same height.

At the slipway the islanders gathered. Gaz had been given a sack of potatoes, eggs, greens, and a bottle of home-brew. He took Sid's hand and shook it hard, hugged him, and too emotional to speak, removed the string with the cockleshell pendant from around his neck and placed it over the boy's head. Hazel and Lo hugged him and he patted Izzi, who yapped in excitement. At the last moment, as Gaz was about to cast off, the dog leaped into the boat.

'Get on out, boy, said Gaz. 'You're not coming along of me.' The dog obeyed, dropping his head in disappointment.

'No, you take Izzi, Gaz,' said Sid. 'He'll help you with the fishing.' He gave the dog a quick hug, and Izzi whined as if he knew that he was leaving Sid here.

'You sure, boy?' the man asked.

Sid nodded and gave the dog a last scratch between his ears. The dog whined softly and gave Sid a paw.

Sid said, 'Go, Izzi, go.' And the dog leapt into the boat and stood at the bow, wagging his tail.

Gaz saluted and nodded a silent thank you as he cast off from the slipway.

The sun was breaking through the morning mist, transforming the fogbound little harbour to a colourful scene of fishing nets and lobster pots, boats bobbing on the opal-green water. Cottages appeared floating in the wreaths of mist. Red seaweeds waved languidly under the water. Oyster-catchers called mournfully as they skimmed the rocks. The sea sparkled like a beaten silver dish. Gaz turned to gaze back at the island. He was looking forward to peace and quiet and getting back to painting. But more importantly, he had to know that Sand, who he and Rose had named Jenny, was safe. If the worst came to the worst and the Reducers came back to the valley, he would take Sand, Stella, and the farmer to the island. As he sailed past the end of the stone pier and the entrance to the harbour he gave one last wave before turning to look towards his goal.

Hazel and Sid clasped hands firmly and stood watching the little boat as it sailed away.

Seven young herring gulls in the mottled brown plumage of their first season followed a powerful adult male. Calling to each other, they flew above the boat towards Land's End.

'Be good, be safe,' called Lo, her voice whisked away by the wind.

Q&A: Ann Kelley discusses *Runners*

What made you choose Cornwall as the setting for Runners?
I have lived in West Cornwall for nearly fifty years, I know it well, the geography, the nature, the climate, the character of the people, so that makes it easy for me to get into the heart of the place in a story. Also, if the worst did happen, as it does in *Runners*, Cornwall would be a fairly easy area to close off from the rest of the country. Lots of Cornish people already think that Cornwall is another country! Our borders are rivers. The bridges could be destroyed, we could shut it off and make it into a fortress, with razor wire and border guards stopping anyone from getting in. It is almost a fortress already. When the railway connection at Dawlish was destroyed by storms early in 2014 we were practically cut off from the rest of the country for six weeks until the track was repaired.

The novel ends on a hopeful note, even thought the future you paint is bleak. Do you really have hope for the future?
That's a difficult question. When I was in my teens there was the threat of nuclear warfare. I dreamed of mushroom clouds, the end of the world. It didn't happen. It seems that every generation has their own bogeyman, its own apocalypse. For this generation it is Global Warming.

However, I read journals like *Scientific American* and *New Scientist,* and books on science and nature. I do believe that ingenuity and man's innate intelligence will produce innovative solutions to the inevitable climate changes that will occur. Mankind will have to adapt or die, like animals, birds and invertebrates. Education is the key. Once we know what the problem is, we can work out how to get around it. Population control is a terrible idea, stopping people from having the families they want, but the world cannot support so many. Or will not be able to, soon enough.

Runners is a way of looking at a possible future in which there is population control. Reading a novel about a possible future gives a chance to think about the future. It is a warning. Oh, dear, that doesn't sound too hopeful, does it? But we have to hold onto hope, but not simply hope, we have to do something positive to help, even if only in a little way. Grow your own food, build a pond for wildlife, recycle

– something simple like that. Walk instead of driving. It all helps. Become a scientist, an inventor, get an education. Don't bury your head in the sand. You'll get sand up your nose!

What makes Sid a survivor?
He's only fourteen years old, and he's having to protect his four-year-old sister, Lolabelle – Lo, who will be killed if she is found by the Reducers. I have found that in a frightening situation, if you have someone more vulnerable to care for, you are suddenly brave and protective. You can face fear and danger in order to save someone else. I think that this is what happens to Sid. His mother's last words to him before she was taken away by soldiers was – 'Take care of my baby.' And he does. And later, when Lo is taken away by the New-Earthers he is desperate to find her. The age difference between them puts him in the position of her carer, and he loves her. He has to survive in order to protect her. Also, he has the natural life-force and physical health of a teen-aged boy that gives him the ability to think ahead, to be innovative, to survive.

By the way, he has an invisible friend – his dead hero, Isambard Brunel, the famous engineer – who sometimes comes to him in times of need and helps him make the right decisions.

You give beautiful, detailed descriptions of the natural world and wild places. Is it right that you have an intense desire for knowledge about nature?
I left school at just seventeen, before my A-levels, got a job at the local library and married at just eighteen. At nineteen I had a chronically sick baby to care for. But I have always read lots of books – novels, and non-fiction. I also write poetry and teach medics and medical students to write poetry. I get them to go into the garden or down to the beach and observe nature closely. Take a flower, a crab, a butterfly, a twig, a spider, and look closely at it. I have done this all my life. I remember being a child lying in long grass, watching beetles and grasshoppers, examining seed heads of grasses, smelling the natural scent of alexanders, watching tadpoles turn into frogs in our tiny pond. The joy of adding to the nature table at school. Bringing fallen nests, shells, pine cones, the dropped tail of a lizard.

Perhaps I should have gone to university and studied zoology or biology. But we weren't taught it well enough at high school to enthuse me to study, and anyway, I couldn't wait to grow up, leave home, have a family.

But now I can read and look and learn all I want about what is all around me. We live on the edge of a sea-cliff, and welcome wildlife, feeding peanuts to badgers by the kitchen door; having a herring gull visit every day, even coming into the house. Feeding small birds, putting up nesting boxes for birds, bats, bees, insects. We have a hedgehog house. It all helps, and I am able to watch, observe, take note, enjoy the natural life that surrounds us.

What do you particularly like about writing for young people?
Between the ages of eleven and eighteen you are open to new ideas and experiences, not cynical, not closed to anything. It's the most exciting and interesting time of life, a time when the decisions you make could benefit or ruin your future. It's a time of experimentation, finding out, listening and learning. Your mind, your brain, is fresh and eager. You are still childlike in your enthusiasm, but adult enough to make sophisticated choices. Who wouldn't want to write for this group of readers?

You can find out more about Ann Kelley at
www.annkelley.co.uk

Also published by **LUATH PRESS**

Last Days in Eden
Ann Kelley
ISBN 978-1-910021-27-9 HBK £9.99

She had made me envious. Strange as it might seem, I had not known envy before. Surely there must be other ways of living, I thought, not hand-to-mouth, alone, in a draughty old shack looking out at the same scene, day after day. Was this to be my future?

An innocent adrift in a world ripped apart by greed and want...

The year is 2137, but the people of Eden are reduced to living in medieval fashion. The human race is deeply divided and the world has been brought to its knees by the Oil Wars and rising sea levels.

Flora is trying to hold on to her humanity as her world changes forever.

Costa Award winning author Ann Kelley's disturbing vision of the future has much to say about our own times.

The Burying Beetle

Ann Kelley

ISBN 978-1-842820-99-5 PBK £9.99
ISBN 978-1-905222-08-7 PBK £6.99

The countryside is so much scarier than the city. It's all life or death here.

Meet Gussie. Twelve years old and settling into her new ramshackle home on a cliff top above St Ives, she has an irrepressible zest for life. She also has a life-threatening heart condition. But it's not in her nature to give up. Perhaps because she knows her time might be short, she values every passing moment, experiencing each day with humour and extraordinary courage.

Gussie's story of inspiration and hope is both heartwarming and heartrending. Once you've met her, you'll not forget her. And you'll never take life for granted again.

Shortlisted for the Branford Boase Award

It is rare to find such tragic circumstances written about without an ounce of self-pity. Rarer still to have the story of a circumscribed existence escaping its confines by sheer force of personality, zest for life.
MICHAEL BAYLEY

The Bower Bird

Ann Kelley

ISBN 978-1-906307-98-1 PBK £6.99

I had open-heart surgery last year, when I was eleven, and the healing process hasn't finished yet. I now have an amazing scar that cuts me in half almost, as if I have survived a shark attack.

Gussie is twelve years old, loves animals and wants to be a photographer when she grows up. The problem is she's unlikely to grow up. Gussie needs a heart and lung transplant, but the donor list is as long as her arm and she can't wait around that long. Gussie has things to do; finding her ancestors, coping with her parents' divorce, and keeping an eye out for the wildlife in her garden.

Winner of the 2007 Costa Children's Book Award.

...lyrical, funny, full of wisdom.
HELEN DUNMORE

...evokes people and places with delicacy, humour and truth – a novel of outstanding beauty
COSTA AWARD JUDGES

Inchworm

Ann Kelley

ISBN 1-906817-12-X PBK £6.99

I ask for a mirror. My chest is covered in a wide tape, so I can't see the clips or incision but I want to see my face, to see if I've changed.

Gussie wants to go to school like every other teenage girl and find out what it's like to kiss a boy. But she's just had a heart and lung transplant and she's staying in London to recover from the operation.

Between managing her parents' love lives, waiting for her breasts to finally start growing, and trying to hide a destructive kitten in her dad's expensive bachelor pad, Gussie makes friends with another cardio patient in the hospital and finds out that she can't have everything her heart desires...

A great book. THE INDEPENDENT

This is definitely one of my top ten books. You have to read it, and it will stay with you forever!
TEEN TITLES

A Snail's Broken Shell

Ann Kelley

ISBN 978-1-906817-40-4 PBK £8.99

What if I had been born with a normal heart and normal everything else? Would I be the same person or has my heart condition made me who I am?

For the first time in years Gussie can run, climb and jump. Every breath she takes is easier now, and every step more confident, but Gussie can't help wondering about her donor. Was she young? Had she been very sick or was there an accident?

And with her new life comes a whole new set of problems. She is going back to school at last – but she doesn't know anyone her own age. With school not meeting up to her expectations, Gussie turns to her old pastimes of birdwatching and photography, but troubling news awaits her there too...

A Snail's Broken Shell is the fourth book in the Costa Award winning Gussie series.

Details of these and other books published by Luath Press can be found at
www.luath.co.uk

Luath Press Limited

committed to publishing well written books worth reading

LUATH PRESS takes its name from Robert Burns, whose little collie
Luath (*Gael.*, swift or nimble) tripped up Jean Armour at a wedding
and gave him the chance to speak to the woman who was to be his wife
and the abiding love of his life. Burns called one of the 'Twa Dogs'
Luath after Cuchullin's hunting dog in Ossian's *Fingal*.
Luath Press was established in 1981 in the heart of
Burns country, and is now based a few steps up
the road from Burns' first lodgings on
Edinburgh's Royal Mile. Luath offers you
distinctive writing with a hint of
unexpected pleasures.

Most bookshops in the UK, the US, Canada,
Australia, New Zealand and parts of Europe,
either carry our books in stock or can order them
for you. To order direct from us, please send a £sterling
cheque, postal order, international money order or your
credit card details (number, address of cardholder and
expiry date) to us at the address below. Please add post
and packing as follows: UK – £1.00 per delivery address;
overseas surface mail – £2.50 per delivery address; overseas airmail –
£3.50 for the first book to each delivery address, plus £1.00 for each
additional book by airmail to the same address. If your order is a gift,
we will happily enclose your card or message at no extra charge.

Luath Press Limited
543/2 Castlehill
The Royal Mile
Edinburgh EH1 2ND
Scotland
Telephone: +44 (0)131 225 4326 (24 hours)
email: sales@luath. co.uk
Website: www. luath.co.uk